THE SPLINTERED COVEN

THE HUMMINGBIRD COVEN

BOOK 3

Copyright © 2026 by Augusta Owens

All rights reserved.

No portion of this book may be reproduced in any form without written permission from the publisher or author, except as permitted by U.S. copyright law.

Contents

The Witch's Press

BREAKING NEWS: Rogue Sea Monster Contained By Schoolchildren, Not Officials
The Witch's Press, Special Dispatch | 12 July

In a stunning turn of events, the rogue sea monster that has wreaked havoc on the Mediterranean Coast for weeks—a maritime terror the Government of Magical or Unusual Creatures (GMUC) had unsuccessfully attempted to cover up—has finally been subdued. But the real shock isn't the creature's capture. It's who did the capturing.

Contrary to earlier reports from the Police Department of Magic (PDM), it was not elite government operatives who brought the creature down. Witnesses and magical tracking logs now confirm that a coven of school-aged children unaffiliated with any official magical authority risked their lives to rescue both the civilians trapped at sea and the operatives who themselves had been overwhelmed, with other reports of siren interference. While it is difficult to pinpoint exactly which agents were present at the scene, evidence points to our very own Council member, Isabel Ortega-Adriano, as a participant in this embarrassing debacle.

The young witches, apparently no older than fourteen, coordinated a complex blend of ancient sea-binding spells and elemental charms—magic that has reportedly not been taught in state-approved curriculums for over a decade. Whether they were wayward students in the wrong place at the right time or quick-thinking citizens stepping in where officials failed, one thing is true: they demonstrated courage beyond their years.

This revelation has sparked widespread concern across magical communities in both the British Isles and the African Union Territories, where tensions have been rising due to recent legislation endangering the rights of magical creatures and unregistered spellcasters. Critics are now demanding an investigation into the GMUC's protocols, training standards, and, most importantly, its continued authority.

"If children can do what trained agents can-

not, perhaps it's time to question who's really protecting us," said Professor Amara Dlamini, a magical ethicist from the Witches' University of Salamanca. "And at what cost to magical beings?"

The defeated sea creature—now identified as an ancient guardian species only seen once before in the last two hundred years—has been disposed of safely. But the political storm brewing in its wake may be even harder to contain.

— J. Lysander Hart, Senior Correspondent, The Witch's Press

Manon

A funeral was held one mid-July morning off of the southern coast of Spain. It was one of those days where the sky had been dull and gray for hours, taunting the attendees with the idea of rain. And yet it refused to fall.

Black fabric draped over Amelia's clammy skin, forming a dress that hung limply past her knees. It was the only black clothing she owned, and it squeezed uncomfortably at her shoulders, the seams worn and faded.

In front of her stood an old woman, her black scarf and clothing flowing in the beach breeze. She spoke with a steady voice in a language Amelia couldn't understand. Not in the literal sense, anyway. She faced towards the coffin, sleek, dark, and perfected down to every angle. It looked like it had been shaped by magic. It probably had. Like most of the attendants, it came from the deep blue sea and there it would return.

When the woman finished her eulogy, four people emerged from the crowd and lifted the coffin with ease, then slowly marched down the slope of the beach. They continued into the water, sinking deeper and deeper until they and the coffin faded from view and the ocean swallowed them whole.

Behind her, Amelia could sense Elena's presence. The witch still smelled of magic potions and failed experiments from that morning, (similar to burned rubber and spoiled milk.) Nevertheless, she'd shown up and paid her respects even though she didn't need to.

Her twin sister Isabel, however, was absent. It seemed that the politician of a witch had more important things to attend to. It wasn't an uncommon occurrence, but Amelia could tell from the downcast look in Sofia's eyes that she was disappointed. Amelia knew all too well what it was to miss her mother. She hadn't seen her own for weeks. Not in person, anyway. Still, it was strange for her to be away from home, especially when home was all the way across the Atlantic ocean. She'd known what the price would be, she reminded herself. She'd known since the day Harriet and Sofia had invited her to practice magic with them, to become part of their coven. And here she was.

Here they all were.

One by one, the rest of the sirens on the beach began to follow Manon's coffin into the ocean, gliding through the gentle waves until their heads duck beneath them, disappearing into the sea foam. It was like a mirage—there one moment, and gone the next. As guilt began to rise up in her like bile, Amelia caught sight of two familiar faces. She gasped.

"Clarisse!" she called over the whooshing of the waves. "Dominique!"

The two sirens paused, their feet submerged in the water. Clarisse, the slighter girl, couldn't have been more than a couple of years older than Amelia herself. Dominique was in her teens, too, but at that moment they both looked so much younger than Amelia had remembered. Hidden in every crevice of their features was Manon, from Clarisse's straight and set nose to Dominique's strong and round shoulders, it was impossible to not see their sister.

There were a million things she could have said to them then. *How are you? Are you okay?* But each one felt more silly than the last.

"What..." Amelia wasn't sure how to ask, but she worried that if she didn't, it would eat at her forever. "What's going to happen to the ship?"

A voice spoke from behind her.

"You can't exactly man a ship without a captain."

It was Peter. Some of his freckles had faded, perhaps from less time spent on the water with the sirens, and the lines of his face seemed to have gotten harsher, but Amelia couldn't tell if his features had really changed so much since she'd last seen him—hardly two weeks ago—or if it was simply a result of his grim expression.

"You're giving up?" Harriet was at Amelia's side, wearing another plain black dress that Sofia had loaned her, and so it was slightly too long for her. "After all the work Manon put towards your cause?"

"It was never my cause," hissed Peter, though he lacked resolve.

"What you do is *important*," said Harriet. She glanced over her shoulder at Elena and the small group of adults waiting on the other side of the sand. "No matter what they say. Or did you forget?"

"It is one thing to risk our lives at sea—against elements with which we are familiar," said Dominique finally, her words tinged with a French accent. "It is another to go against your kind." She gazed out at the water before directing her soft voice back towards the witches. "Do not doubt that we will honor our sister, but do not criticize how we choose to do so. Goodbye, Hummingbird Coven."

With that, the two sisters turned and followed after the rest of their pod, becoming one with the ocean's waves.

"Cowards," said Harriet to no one in particular before stomping away.

Amelia turned to Peter. "I'm sorry," she said, even if it might not have meant anything to him, because it was true.

"Yeah," he sighed, "I know you are." And then he walked away, too.

In the distance, she could see two figures, a boy and a girl standing at the edge of the water. The tall and lanky boy seemed to catch sight of Amelia and slowly waved a hand to her. Fran and Yolanda then crouched down towards the sand until their forms began to warp and shudder, brown skin turning into blue and green scales that stretched over their now reptilian bodies. And then they, too, were lost to the sea.

Amelia had forgotten to wave back to him. He must hate her, she thought. He must hate all of them.

Amelia had a persistent headache. Ever since they'd returned from the funeral, there had been a low hum in the back of her skull, and though she tried to ignore it, the feeling wouldn't budge.

She had to admit, when she'd been told that she was leaving her home to go study witchcraft in the south of Spain and finally master her magical gift, she'd had some high expectations. But instead of flying through the air on a broom or dancing naked around a bonfire, she was sitting at the dining table, a pen in her hand as she tried to memorize a dozen words in Latin that all kind of meant the same thing.

"No, Sam, not '*uh*'. It's more of an '*oo*' sound. And Harry, dear, keep working on your stressed syllables," Elena directed.

"I thought we were going to practice offensive spells this morning," complained Harriet, scratching out another line of text in her notebook.

Elena continued scribbling words in the air with her finger, each glowing red stroke lingering in the open space until fading away once the girls had copied them down. "You've yet to master the defensive. Let's not get ahead of ourselves. Now, the nominative plural..."

"We've been doing defensive for *weeks!* What more is there to learn?"

"Oh, Harry," laughed Elena, pausing her scribbling. "If you're going to excel as a witch, you must know that there is *always* more to learn. Anyway, until all three of you have mastered a skill, we won't move on to the next level. Might I remind you that you're still a coven and you will train like one."

Harriet flashed a look at Amelia and Sam.

"Don't look at me," muttered Sam as she copied down her declensions. "Elena said my caster runes were *perfecto.*"

"*Perfectas*," corrected Elena. "How about a Spanish lesson later this afternoon?"

Sam groaned.

"But she's right," blurted Amelia. "Don't you think it would be nice for us to know some offensive spells? Especially with...everything that's, you know, *happened?*"

Their mentor looked down at her almost pitifully. "Don't tell me you're still worried about that, *cariño.*"

"Of course I'm still worried. We all are."

The words floating in the air dissipated and Elena lowered her hand. "Well, then. I have said this before but I will say it again, and let it be known that I say it with absolute confidence. Here it is. Are you ready? It's quite simple."

Her pupils leaned in.

"Everything will be completely and utterly *fine.*" Happy smatterings of light glittered around her hands. "If I could go into detail about every meticulous procedure performed by the GMUC at this very moment with the sole purpose of ensuring your safety, I would, but I have neither the time nor the jurisdiction, so trust me when I tell you, the GMUC *will* handle it."

She leaned forward over the table and gestured earnestly. "Trained operatives are tracking your late grandmother—the version of her that isn't late—as we speak. If she steps foot in this timeline again, it'll be the last thing she ever does!" She laughed lightly and then seemed to realize exactly what she was saying. "Forgive my morbidity. But after all, you girls have me, don't you? And I would never put you in harm's way."

Harriet and Sofia exchanged a dubious glance.

But Amelia had more to say. "I still don't see how that's a reason to not teach us the things we're all going to learn anyway."

"All in good time," replied Elena. "None of your peers got shortcuts or special treatment."

Suddenly, Sam blurted, "None of them had to watch their friends die in front of them either."

All the air was instantly sucked out of the room.

For a moment, Elena was dumbfounded, and then she sighed.

"That's enough. Why don't we all take our *siesta* and tomorrow—"

"No!" cried Amelia. "She's right. Elena. You have to see that she's right. We can't all just sit here, waiting for her to come back!"

"We are *safe* here—" began Elena, her voice rising.

"That's a lie and you know it."

"Amelia, go to your room." The witch looked physically pained now. The rest of the coven was just watching them in a mix of awe and concern, a distinct bead of sweat forming at Sofia's hairline.

Amelia stood, her chair hitting the bookshelf behind her with a *bang*. "No! You can't just shut us out and make us—" She swung her hand through the air without thinking and all at once the notebooks and pens sitting on the dining room table were catapulted into the air and scattered across the room. Their cups of water and the tablecloth went with them, splashing liquid over their laps.

The girls cried out and ducked for cover. But it was over as soon as it began.

Amelia was frozen.

Elena, her gaze now cold, held up a finger. A pen levitated inches from her eye, the deadly sharp tip focused on her iris. Without drawing her gaze from Amelia once, she lazily lowered her hand and the pen floated back onto the table.

Amelia's mouth had fallen open in shock. She had to force it closed and gulped nervously, taking in the damage around her. Her fingertips still buzzed with magic, purple mist dematerializing around her hands. "I didn't mean to do that," she managed to choke out.

Before anyone else could speak, she turned and ran out of the house. With a purple stain burned into the edges of her vision, as if her magic was still trying to absorb her from all angles, she fished her bicycle out of the garage, swatting away the summer spiders. Then she rode away while straining to recall the route she desired.

Although they'd been living here long enough for her to learn some basic Spanish vocabulary like *gofre* (which meant waffle, because it was hard to get a good pancake there that wasn't actually just a crepe) and *chocolate* (which meant chocolate), she had never had a strong sense of direction and had gotten lost among the twists and turns of the narrow roads in the small town more than once.

Miraculously, she arrived where she'd meant to without making a turn into the river, and tied her bike up at a pole before strolling into the tiny café and falling into a seat with exhaustion.

"Right, um, a *gofre con chocolate, por favor,*" she said to the waitress who somehow already knew her name and had already begun writing her order on a notepad before she even said it.

Once the woman was gone, Amelia let her head fall to the table, breathing deeply as she tried to calm the magic still prickling at her fingertips. It was like there was a creature inside of her, an indescribable force just waiting to be released.

She'd known the effects that a magic surge could have on a witch once they united with their coven and Elena had warned her that because Amelia wasn't introduced to magic until late, it may hit her slower and stronger than it had with Sofia and Harriet. But the magic wasn't the hard part. She was learning how to use it, how to manipulate it. The hard part was keeping it locked inside her, repressing that deep purple glow down in her chest, squeezing it tight until—

"Amelia, is that you?"

She turned and was met with a vaguely familiar face walking towards her (with such a bounce in her step that she was nearly skipping—as usual) and beaming with joy. The girl took off her heart-shaped sunglasses and squealed lightly with a Spanish accent, "I haven't seen you since your birthday!"

This was a girl Sofia had invited to the party along with a few of the other witches and casters from school. Her name was Roni and she'd seemed to enjoy the party. They'd all blown out candles, eaten cake, and played music in an attempt to prove that nothing was wrong.

"Yeah. A whole week ago," replied Amelia as she was wrapped into a hug.

"So, how are you?" Roni asked eagerly.

"Fine. Yeah, great," Amelia lied.

"Oh, I'm glad!" the girl exclaimed before helping herself to the seat across from Amelia. Roni had a sort of enthusiasm that Amelia had only seen before in Sam, however Roni's version wasn't as endearing. "I know you all are probably still training. It must be hard."

Amelia wasn't sure if the observation was meant to be condescending or genuinely sympathetic. Roni, Amelia assumed, had started her own training at thirteen, like most witches.

"It's fine," Amelia said again. "Elena's a good teacher."

"My mother says she's a lunatic," said Roni, "but I know better."

"O-kay...."

"So, how is Sam?"

"She's fine," Amelia said for the third time now.

"Good! You know, we should all go out one day. It would be fun."

Just then, the waitress came with her waffle and set it down in front of them. "*Gracias,*" said Amelia.

"Ooh! Can I have some?" asked Roni.

Amelia blinked. "Sure."

The girl scooped a piece into her mouth and then, with her mouth full, spoke again. "So, what do you think? About going out?"

"Sounds fun," she replied without much thought as she took her own bite. The taste of sugar immediately calmed her senses, and she felt the magic at her fingertips ease away at last. "Yeah, really fun."

"Great! I can invite Oscar and you can invite Sam."

Amelia paused with her fork inches from her mouth, wracking her memory before a face appeared in her mind of a boy they had met at the night of the bonfire; a boy she'd never really spoken to. "Oscar?" she asked skeptically. "Why Oscar?"

"Well, he was asking about her," said Roni as she wiped the chocolate from her mouth with a napkin. "I think they are cute together, no?"

Amelia was at a loss for words, her mouth agape.

"Anyway, I have to go," Roni sighed as she stood. She leaned down and gave Amelia a tight hug. "But thank you for the food. We'll see each other later. Bye-bye!"

Then Amelia was left alone, suddenly feeling much too sick to finish her waffle.

Elena's Illusion

Crickets chirped around the witches and darkness drew across the fields before them. Amelia was tired of staying up late for lessons, and as the weather grew warmer and the days longer, it was later and later when they ventured out, but Elena insisted. "This way, it's easier to see your glow," she explained. "That's very important for getting in touch with your inner magic and grounding yourself, yes? Besides, if anyone sees you, it will merely seem like fireworks."

All that logic aside, Amelia was strictly a morning person, and right now, all that called to her was her warm bed.

"Not to mention," Elena continued, "it's much too hot at this time of year to be running in the sun."

"Running?" Amelia was queasy already.

"Remember, your body is just as important as your magic. Imagine if you're among iron, and all you have are your fists." She raised her own to illustrate the point.

"Does that mean we'll finally get to fight each other?" asked Harriet, eyes narrowing.

"Don't get excited," quipped Sofia, sitting down on a comically large squash. (Which had probably not been so large before she came along.) "What are we in for tonight?" she asked her aunt, who was looking more enthusiastic by the second.

"I am so glad you asked, Sofi." With that, Elena raised her arms and, in one grand motion, swept them across the open fields. At first, the crops shuddered with the movement, and Amelia feared the woman was about to trigger an earthquake, but then the world around them began to move in a different way.

The darkness of the sky seemed to melt away along with the stars, slowly transforming into an abstract smattering of gray. The sky was turning to stone and Amelia watched in amazement as it slowly wrapped around her, closing in on all sides with an unnerving crunch. Something clicked into place and she gasped.

She found herself in a narrow opening, a strange sort of cave with a curved stone ceiling and bumpy dirt floors, illuminated by burning golden sconces on either wall. The only way out seemed to be forward; down the dark hall where the emptiness and silence stretched on.

For a moment, she thought it appropriate to panic. But it was only Elena, she reminded herself. Her and her strange talent for illusions—although it was all unsettlingly realistic. At the edge of her vision, if she really focused, there was a familiar red glow, Elena's aura peaking through the mist.

Not real, she reminded herself.

She waved a hand in front of her face to see her palm. She flipped her hand to see the burned scar on the back of it, a distantly painful reminder of the past. That was real. It was only her surroundings that were an illusion. She tried not to think too much into it.

"Okay," she whispered to herself, heart racing. "Defensive magic. Gotta defend." Whatever Elena had in store, it couldn't be much worse than what they'd already faced. She bared her fists and took a step forward. She cast sideways glances to every candlelight flicker, waiting for something to come jumping out of the shadows. A fork appeared in the path, dividing into three, each more or less the same. Just as she was about to move towards the middle path, she heard a distant cry, a desperate noise from a voice she recognized clearly.

"Sofia." She abandoned the middle path and darted towards the point where she'd heard the noise. But it was a dead end. *What?* She spun around, almost sure the sound had come from this spot, but her thoughts were interrupted.

There were two golden eyes, distinct against the shadowed corner up ahead. A thrill of fear prickled through her. *It's not real, it's not real.*

The creature's form blended into the shadows, and even as it crept forward, it was difficult to make it out. The candle on the sconce flared, illuminating deep black fur spread across shifting shoulder blades like a dark blanket thrown over a pile of bones floating in water. Below those fiery eyes were two rows of gleaming teeth, even sharper than its menacing gaze. It was a wolf, but not like any wolf that Amelia had ever seen. It was too large, too sharp and angled, like a nightmare drawn from memory.

Elena and her wicked imagination, Amelia cursed to herself.

It's not real. The thought continued its echoing as she raised her hands, palms open towards the creature, who did not stir at her movement. *It's not real.* She drew the magic within her up through her chest, imagined that purple glow, and tried to remember the smell of honey and amber. Her trigger.

The purple glow at her palms intensified, the magic within her awaking, and *boy* was it happy to be set free. It had been waiting to be liberated from the confines of her hands.

Amelia recalled their weeks of lessons, everything Elena had taught her about defensive magic in the classroom. She envisioned a shield around herself, sliding her hands flat across the space in front of her, as if there were already a wall there that separated her from the wolf.

She took a breath, and as she exhaled, the wolf lunged.

Her eyes closed and magic burst from her hands, almost knocking her backwards, but when she looked up, she saw the terrifying creature clawing at the empty air in front of it. *Not empty*, she corrected herself. A faint purple glimmer tinted the barrier. Her shield had materialized.

"*Yes!*" she cried, pumping her fist in the air, and as soon as she did, the dejected creature ceased its clawing at the invisible barrier and vanished out of sight. As her shoulders relaxed, so did the shield. And then it was over.

Looking around, she called out into the emptiness, "Am I done now?" Her voice echoed back to her, which—when she really thought about it—shouldn't have been possible. The walls were only an illusion, after all. One thing was irrevocably true: as bonkers as Elena may have been, she was just as talented.

No reply came, and so Amelia accepted the answer was probably "no". She sighed and continued forward. Now, where was it that she'd heard Sofia—?

Something at the end of the narrow cave caught her eye. A figure, tall and thin, hovering somewhere in the middle of the path. Its feet did not touch the ground, and it seemed to sway idly from one side to the other. Its face was covered by a shroud, loose threads hanging off of its body.

She stumbled back. It wasn't one of her covenmates. It wasn't Elena, either. It was too uncanny, too unhuman. Whatever it was, it was part of Elena's tests. Which meant that it wasn't real. And Amelia was in no real danger. *Right?*

A low hum seemed to emanate from the figure. It had no visible face, no eyes to see with. But it could see her. Somehow, she knew it could see her.

She raised her hands again. "Come on," she urged. She wanted to get it over with, swallowing her fear so it formed a tight lump in her throat.

The figure responded, floating down the path with an eerie determination. As it grew nearer, she could hear it whisper, low breathy voices coming from behind its shroud, each one overlapping the other. The whispers grew louder and louder, impossible to discern its words. Amelia's heart was pounding in her chest and the world seemed to darken around her, the candles snuffing out one by one as the horrid creature passed by them.

"No," she gasped, breath hitching. The whispers were nearly deafening, piercing through her skull. Her muscles weakened and dread overtook her.

It was a trick. Victoria had tricked them. She'd been waiting in the shadows for this moment so she could attack, and now they were supposed to believe that they were safe. But they *weren't*. The monster was real. It had to be. Nothing that was truly an illusion could be so—

Without realizing it, Amelia had allowed her magic to rise within her again. Her glow had returned and the shroud was illuminated by her fire. She screamed and it burst from within her. A force repelled the creature away from her, ripped from her chest. When the magic reached the creature, it was over as soon as it began. The force obliterated it instantly, smothering it into dust.

Her glow was blinding. She had to take a step back, covering her face, and when she looked back up, coughing, she was no longer in the cave.

It was night again and she was standing in the open field, leafy crops licking at her legs. The lights of the town glittered in the distance on the round hill. Amelia turned, looking for the dreadful creature. "Where is it? Where—Where did it go?"

But it was Elena that stood before her, her arms crossed and expression as stern as Amelia had ever seen.

Amelia was at a loss for words. She looked around again, and found Harriet and Sofia standing a few feet away, both looking mildly confused. But there was no whispering ghost to be found. And no Victoria. "I...I don't understand."

"Amelia," Elena began. "We agreed on defensive magic. That includes shields and the occasional telekinetic push, but only spells that put distance between you and your attacker. We did *not* agree on what you just did."

Amelia looked down at her hands. "I didn't mean to."

Elena leaned down to be at level with her. "Intentions are important, dear. They are. But they don't matter quite so much as actions. I wish it wasn't that way, but it is."

"But that...*thing*. It was doing something. Like, sucking the energy from me."

Elena shook her head. "It was only an illusion. It couldn't *do* anything."

But she had felt dread overtake her, something as strong as any other kind of magic. Something stronger than fear alone.

Elena patted her on the shoulder, and then stood upright again to speak to the other witches. "You all must be prepared for surprises. And that means you must rely on more than your traditional senses."

"Well, what else is there?" Harriet huffed. She brushed dirt off the butt of her pants, meaning that her session had probably gone just about as bad as Amelia's.

Elena sighed. "Harry, you took just about every wrong turn away from Amelia and Sofi, despite the fact that I lit up each correct path a little bit more for you. What you need to focus on is *sticking with your team*. Understood?"

Harriet twisted her lips in distaste.

Elena went on. "Sofia, while I appreciate you thinking outside of the box and summoning your vines through the ground, you must remember that not everything can be solved with just your natural talent." Sofia looked down at the ground, her cheeks flushed. "Especially considering that if you were in a *real* cave, you might not have so much life in the soil below to work with." Elena gestured to the vines that had crept through the surface of the ground at Sofia's side, reaching up even taller than the girl herself. "In reality, you summoned plants from about the most fertile soil there is, so it's no wonder you were successful. Let's work on your reaction time."

"Yes, *tía*," replied Sofia.

Finally, Elena turned back to Amelia. "And you fell for a very simple trick. You followed Sofia's cry for help."

Amelia looked at her incredulously. "Well, what was I supposed to do? Harry messed up because she ignored the rest of us and I messed up because I *didn't?*"

Elena smiled knowingly, then pointed to Sofia. "Sofi was on your left, all the way over there when the illusion began. But the sound came from your right, not that much longer after she went out of sight. Do you understand? She would have had to have moved all the way across the field within seconds, and all without passing by you. If you would have taken a moment to think, you would have realized that before walking yourself into a dead end."

Amelia was getting more and more frustrated. "I mean, she could've...I don't know..."

"It's not just about logic," Elena continued. "Once you feel more in touch with your magic, you'll be able to sense when your covenmates are near. You'll sense your own magic getting stronger with their proximity."

Amelia paused, and finally conceded, looking down at her feet and nodding.

Elena took her chin in her hand and spoke in a tone low enough that the other witches couldn't hear. "Nothing is more important than your coven, Amelia. Remember that. They are the basis of everything you will ever do."

With that, the woman sighed and turned away. She suddenly seemed much more tired. She began to tread slowly back towards the house, her breath heavy with exhaustion as she called the witches back inside.

"Hey," Harriet came up behind Amelia. "I thought Sam was gonna come out with us tonight."

"Oh." Amelia was taken off guard. "Yeah, um. I think she was too tired or something. She's probably in bed."

Harriet gave her a funny look and sauntered off.

A Different Kind of Magic

The truth was, nobody had actually asked Sam if she wanted to come out that night while the witches trained. The even sadder truth was that she wasn't even sure if she wanted to. Regardless, Sam did not sleep until late that night. She didn't do anything really, except sit in her bed, watching as purple, green, and red colors flashed through the window. A dull pain weighed down on her until she sunk into the covers, covering her eyes with her sheets. When Amelia finally did come to bed, opening the door with a cautious creak, neither of them said anything. Sam considered saying something, but when she heard Amelia get into the bed opposite, she figured they were both probably too tired to speak anyway.

The next morning they didn't talk much either, but that was okay. Sam already had other plans.

Getting out of the house proved much easier than she'd thought, and certainly much easier than if she were still living at home. When the four girls groggily made their way to the kitchen, they found nothing but a sticky note left on the counter from Elena that she had left to meet with her covenmates, Rozalia and Eleanor, and that she would return later that night.

"What do you think they're doing?" asked Amelia.

"Sometimes they just need to reconnect," Sofia explained. "You know how witches get when they're away from their covens."

"She did seem pretty tired last night," Amelia remarked. "Do you think it was magic?"

Sofia shrugged. "When you're separated for that long, anything can happen. I'm sure she just needs to recharge."

"A warning would have been nice," said Harriet.

"When your coven needs you, they need you." Sofia walked away nonchalantly.

"I guess," Harriet muttered.

The nice thing was that there was no adult to question her when Sam slipped out the back door without a word. It wasn't that she wanted to separate herself from the other witches. In fact, it was the opposite. Sam had watched her coven train day after day, learning spells and magic in a way that she could just not comprehend. She knew that if she left all her own training up to Elena, she would never advance in the same way. It just wasn't plausible. And Sam had frankly grown tired of watching the world work around her while she stayed in place.

And then again, thought Sam as she squeezed her way through the narrow gap in the fence, held together by a heavy metal chain and lock, she'd never been much of a rule follower anyway.

"There she is!" a voice called.

Sam looked up and was met with a small group of people about her age. They waited down below her where the ground dipped into a concrete bowl. The abandoned skate rink had probably been nice at one point in time with its hills and ramps that made her dizzy just to look at, but now it was more like an empty husk. The concrete was covered with moss, vines, and crunchy dead leaves in every crevice and the fence that blocked off the area around it was so weak that it rattled in the wind.

The person who had spoken was Adelheid, a girl with pale skin and jet black hair that sort of made her look like how Sam would have imagined vampires to look before meeting Gloria. However, once she came closer, she could see the way the girl's eyes lit up warmly, her words laced with a slight German accent as she said, "I was worried you didn't get my message."

"No, I got it," Sam assured, reaching deep into her jeans pocket, which held far more space than any pocket should have been able to hold. Once she was elbow deep, she got a hold of what she was looking for and pulled out a small frog. "You know, I thought you guys sent messages with owls."

Adelheid gently took the frog from her, cupping her hands over its body as it made a squeaking *ribbit*. "My mother's familiar. He's very reliable."

The small amphibian opened its mouth again, but this time instead of a frog noise, it was Adelheid's voice that left its throat. *"Good morning, Sam. The other Caster's and I are meeting up tomorrow at the old abandoned skate rink and I thought you might want to—"*

"Enough of that," said Adelheid before closing the creature's mouth, silencing her own message, and dropping it to the ground. It went leaping out of sight as Sam nervously wiped the residual frog slime onto her shorts. "Introductions are in order."

"Right," said Sam, looking over at the other Casters with them, some faces familiar and some not.

"You remember Emily," said Adeleid, pointing to the English girl with bright blue eyes and short locks that curled around her ears.

"We met at the bonfire," Sam remembered. "You're in Roni's coven."

Emily nodded contently. "She couldn't make it."

"Too good to hang out with some lousy Casters, I'm sure." That was the boy standing beside Emily, who looked vaguely familiar to Sam, although she couldn't quite place his face. He was taller than the girls, but something about him gave her the impression that he wasn't all that much older.

"Stop it, Oscar," huffed Emily, twirling a strand of her hair.

"This is Naiara," Adelheid continued, gesturing to the next girl with knowing almond eyes lined in black and a sort of playful grin. "She's a Caster, too."

"Nice to meet you," the girl said with a nod.

"And obviously you know Oscar," said Adelheid.

Sam feigned agreement. "Um. Right."

Oscar spoke up again. "So, you've finally decided to come over to the dark side."

"Oh, I think she has," agreed Adelheid.

"I want to be a Caster," stated Sam, quieting them. "I want to do magic like you all. But I want to do it on my own terms. I'm tired of Latin lessons and waiting for Elena to have time for me when she's already dealing with the other witches." She wanted to say more, tell them why she felt such urgency now because of what they'd gone through in Melilla, but nobody knew the full truth of what had happened except for them and the GMUC. And besides, the last thing she wanted was to worry them. It wasn't like Victoria would ever come for them, too.

"I understand," said Naiara. "All I wanted when I turned thirteen was to start practicing magic like all my cousins.

I bought my own cauldron before I could even say proper incantations." She giggled reminiscently.

Sam couldn't imagine what it must have been like for them, the girls in witch families who never activated their witch gene, who never found their coven when they turned thirteen, who never received a coven book or natural talent. She supposed that was why being a Caster was so important to these girls. But Sam didn't want to be a Caster to make up for something she lacked. She didn't want to be a Caster just because she couldn't be anything else. Something had called her out here. Some feeling rooted deep down within her told her that this was the answer.

"You came to the right place," said Adelheid, a mischievous glint in her eye. She fanned out her fingers and something sparked between them, revealing a tiny glass jar. "Some people think that Casters don't have what it takes for the magical world, that all we do is copy witches, that we want to be exactly like them. I mean, over two hundred types of magical beings are recognized in the GMUC as of today, but there are thirteen spots on the council and *every* place is filled with either a witch, vampire, or elf? *One* elf, mind you—"

"You and your politics," groaned Emily, who was notably the only witch there. "You're going to talk her ear off."

Adelheid shot her a look before continuing. "Anyway, this is not the case. We Casters have our *own* culture, our own methods. And we're just as dangerous as anyone else." With that, she popped open the cork of her little jar and poured the ash-like contents into her hand, and drew something into the surface of her palm. She made a fist and blew through the gap in her fingers. As the ash flew away, so did she. In a moment, she had turned to dust.

Sam watched in amazement as Adelheid appeared again at her side, and then again behind her, and then again at the top of the skate rink, looking down on them all.

"That's incredible!" Sam exclaimed.

The girl with the eyeliner, Naiara, laughed. "That's nothing." She plucked a matchstick from her pocket and struck it against the concrete ground. It came alight in a bright green flame, lighting up her smug smile. "Teleporting is nice, but don't you want to see it *twice?*" Then with the matchstick she drew two identical runes in the air in front of her where they left behind a trail of green smoke. She looked back at the others and blew a kiss, the flame going out with it. After that, she stepped through one of the runes and came out the other—At least, one of her did.

Sam wasn't seeing double. Two Naiara's now stood before her. They both winked in unison.

"Is it an illusion?" asked Sam, thinking of Elena's natural talent. But in response, both of the Naiara's before her reached forward and tapped her on the shoulder, solid and real. And a little bit creepy. "Now, that's..." Sam was at a loss for an adjective that did it justice.

"I know," said Naiara. Both of them, actually. But after a couple seconds, the doppelganger faded into obscurity and so did the runes.

Emily squealed with delight. "We need the roller skates!" She ran off to the other side of the rink with such a bounce to her step that she was nearly skipping and disappeared around a corner before retrieving an old cardboard box that was disintegrating around the edges. It looked just as neglected as everything else in the rink. Emily dropped the box in front of them, then raised her hands. When she did, all five pairs of roller skates floated up and out of the box, then shot towards each person one by one.

Sam's pair of skates came at her so fast it nearly hit her in the chest, but suddenly Oscar jumped in front of her and caught them midair before they could collide. He handed them to her gently. "D'you know how to get them working?"

"Oh, yeah. I did figure skating when I was little." Sam began to strap them on.

"No," laughed Oscar. "I mean, like, *working.*"

Across from them, Adelheid and Naiara had already tied on their skates and were drawing more symbols in the ground in front of them. They stepped into the symbols and shot off into the air, gliding along the concrete on their jet-fast skates. Adeleid whooped and screamed with delight, making loop-de-loops over the ramps and ridges of the rink as a blaze of smoke followed behind her. Naiara zoomed past them, her hair blowing in the wind with a careless grace while she twisted and turned.

That is so fricking cool, Sam thought. Her heart pulsated with excitement. "Show me, please."

Oscar, to her surprise, took her hand and sprinkled salt into it. "You have to draw two different glyphs. First, one with salt. This'll keep you protected so you don't fall on your bum or get out of control." He guided her hand to the ground and drew a strange symbol in the ground with the salt. "Just like that. Now we make another rune with ashrite." He pulled out another chalky mixture and helped her draw a second symbol. "You can put on the skates now, but be careful because they're already charmed. The laces are talisman thread so be gentle with 'em."

"If they're already charmed, why do we need the second rune?"

"That's Caster magic for you. Nothing's cut and dry like witchcraft." He tilted his head. "Unless you find the shortcuts."

Sam raised an eyebrow and tightened the laces. "Now what?"

He extended an arm. "Step through the salt, then the ashrite rune."

She carefully did as he said, and then, as she shifted her weight forward, pushing back on her heel, she jolted forward with overwhelming force. The wind hit her in the face so harshly that she gasped for air, an overexcited laugh caught in her throat. "Oh my *goooooosh!*" she cried, whipping past Oscar and sailing up the curving ramp. She went up and up until gravity stalled and she went falling back down again. She tried to twist midair, bending the skates to her will, but she reacted a moment too late and made contact with the concrete.

For a moment, she thought she'd been terribly hurt, sliding down the curve on her knees, but to her own shock, she was still laughing. The joyful noise escaped her against her will. She wasn't injured. Not even bruised. "The salt worked!"

Oscar stood above her and lended a hand.

"You doubted me?"

"A little." She took his hand and carefully rose to her feet. "Let's do it again."

They continued like that for hours, leaping and sailing through open air under the blistering summer sun. When Sam started to get tired, the Casters produced what looked to be a sort of homemade fruit leather that when eaten, substituted an eight-hour sleep. They argued with each other on whose recipe was better. Emily insisted Adelheid's was the most effective, but Naiara's tasted better. Sam agreed that taste triumphed all.

But as they fought, played, and laughed until they couldn't breathe, something was eating at Sam, some feeling that she couldn't identify. It was like she was meant to be realizing something, but wasn't yet sure what. She was happy, she was *alive.* So why was she still thinking of Amelia, Harriet, and Sofia? It wasn't like they'd be lost without her. In fact, Sam imagined they were probably practicing their own magic right then at that moment, having the time of their lives just like she was.

Because she was. She was having the time of her life.

Totally.

The Coven That Was Absolutely Completely One Hundred Percent Fine

Amelia was about to lose her mind.

"Why would she have just *left* without saying a word? Are you guys sure she didn't leave a note? Did you check the kitchen?"

"You checked the kitchen twice," Sofia reminded her. "Maybe she just went for a walk."

"In this weather?" asked Harriet, who was sitting directly in front of the electric fan. Being English, she was the least accustomed to the summer heat that plagued them now. She was also determined to make that everyone else's problem for the remainder of the season. "Maybe she couldn't take it. Ran off to Antarctica to escape the heat wave."

"There is no heat wave," said Sofia. "We're in Spain."

"Global warming," sighed Harriet, leaning her head back over the edge of the couch.

Amelia was biting her already short nails. "I think we should be looking for her. What if something bad happened?"

Sofia wrapped an arm around her. "Amelia, it's *okay*. Sam is fine."

Amelia forced herself to take a breath. Sofia was probably right. And besides, Amelia trusted Sam! She did. Really. She could be very logical about this. Though a whispering anxiety chewed at the back of her brain, the hushed sound of Victoria's name repeated over and over again, she could resist her impulses.

"Yeah." Slowly, Amelia settled down onto the couch beside Harriet, who didn't look at all pleased to be sharing her space.

"This isn't about your evil grandma again, is it?" asked Harriet. "What? Don't look at me like that, Sofi. She's being ridiculous."

"She has a right to be nervous."

"Oh, so *now* you think she should be nervous."

"That's not what I said."

"It's what you think."

Amelia turned to Sofia. "Is that true?"

The girl's eyes wandered with increasing discomfort. "No—Well. Yes. I mean no. Not really."

Harriet grinned. "This is gonna be good." That earned her another sour look from her covenmate.

"You've stayed quiet this whole time, Sofi," Amelia pointed out. "You saw all the same things we did. So what do you really think? About Elena not teaching us some real magic, telling us everything is fine, the fact that we haven't heard *anything* about Victoria?"

The girl pursed her lips and carefully leaned against the couch edge. The internal conflict waging in her mind was easily visible to them both. "Well," she began hesitantly. "Well, if I really had to answer, I'd say that it's probably...maybe...possibly...not the most convincing reassurance that I've heard."

"*Hah!*" exclaimed Harriet.

Just then the door opened and Sam walked in. They all paused and she looked around confusedly. "Hi."

The awkward silence that followed was palpable.

"Where were you?" Harriet was the first to ask.

Amelia knew full well that Sam was an atrocious liar, and so—to her dismay—she was certain that the next words to leave her lips were completely true.

"Some of the Casters from school invited me out. We went...um...roller skating."

"Which Casters?" asked Sofia, not at all accusatorily.

"Just Adelheid, Emily, Naiara, and Oscar."

Amelia sat a bit straighter. "Oscar?"

"Yeah." Sam glanced around. "He's nice." With that, she walked off to her room and shut the door behind her.

For perhaps the first time in all of Amelia's fourteen years of life, she had no idea what her best friend was thinking.

That night the moon—not quite full—had taken upon itself to cast the fields in a sapphire blue. Behind the witches' house, the water in the swimming pool glistened mesmerizingly, each droplet sparkling in a gorgeous mess of reflections and refractions.

Amelia stepped out, holding a jar of water from the sink. She set it down by the pool and tightened the lid. Tonight she had been tasked with this job, and it would be her who would have to come back and retrieve it before dawn. Elena had told them that the moon water could be used to make healing potions over a cauldron later, but they hadn't quite gotten that far in their studies yet, so she was stuck with the simpler chores.

She paused by the pool and slowly neared the edge, not thinking about it much. The reflection that stared back at her resembled stained glass, but it was wobbled and warped. The image was practically unrecognizable, her in a T-shirt that hung as far as her knees and ratty old sleep shorts, a frizzy puff of hair atop her head, and bags under her eyes.

She held a hand out and bit her lip, imagining the magic within her focus into a tiny pinpoint that settled right atop the pool water. She strained to contain it, gritting her teeth as her aura began to flow through her in a dull purple.

And then the water's rippling came to a stop. Even though the wind still blew, even though the pool's motors still whirred below, the water had paused as if to say, *well, all you had to do was ask.*

"It's kinda too late for a swim," said someone from behind her. Amelia would have recognized that voice every time.

Sam came up to join her at her side. Amelia must have gotten distracted because the water had started moving again. "Is it?" she countered.

Sam shrugged.

Without warning, something compelled Amelia, and so she took a step forward. Gravity dropped from beneath her and her body crashed into the water. It wasn't as cold as she'd expected; it had been warmed from the sun of the day before.

She stayed beneath the surface for a moment, a bubble of breath contained in her cheeks.

There was a loud crash to her left and Amelia turned, squinting to see Sam's shadow swimming at her side. She rose to the surface and they finally faced each other again.

Sam's hair was slicked back against her neck when she rose up out of the water. The droplets falling over her cheeks looked like glitter, dripping off her lower lip like honey. She was so blue, and not just from the moon. Today, Sam had seemed to take on a different hue completely, and Amelia saw her then in a way she never had before.

"Sam."

"Yeah?"

Amelia wasn't at all sure what she had been planning to say. She didn't even remember deciding to say her name out loud. And so she had to make something up so that she didn't seem absolutely bonkers.

"The moon is so pretty."

However, that just made her seem dumb.

Sam craned her head upwards to see it. Amelia's eyes followed the curve of her exposed neck. "It's almost a full moon. I love full moons. Even before the whole witch thing. My mom really loved them, too. She used to take us out to an empty parking lot and we'd just..." she sighed, spreading her arms across the water, "relax."

It was rare that Sam spoke about her mother, but Amelia knew most of the story. She had died when Sam was little, but not little enough to forget. Sometimes the way she talked about it seemed secretive or hesitant, but Amelia suspected it was simpler than that. The memories themselves were hazy. Whenever Sam brought up snippets like these, it was like they were both hearing them for the first time, like they were both wandering through Sam's mind, hand in hand.

When Amelia looked back at Sam her expression had shifted into something harsher, a crease on her brow. Now that look, she knew. That was the look of a painful memory bubbling to the surface, a recent one. It had become more prevalent since the night at the creek with Matthew, Sam's father. Amelia waited for a moment, allowing her space to speak if she wanted to, but the crease in her brow smoothed over on its own. Perhaps it was getting easier.

"Do you miss her?" Amelia ventured to ask.

"In a way." She had to think for a while and was silent for another minute. "I guess, in a way that I feel like she should be here. That it feels wrong that she's not. Is that how you miss someone?"

"I can't think of any other definition."

"Yeah." Another beat. "It's more than that, though. I get this feeling that I'm not where I'm supposed to be. Like I must've...taken a wrong turn, or...put my shoes on the wrong feet—Oh, I just realized I got in the pool with shoes on."

Amelia would have laughed but she was too distracted by her last words. A creeping anxiety prickled at the back of her neck and she was trying to keep dread from making its way through her. "You really feel like you're in the wrong place?"

Sam opened her mouth then closed it again. "I don't know. I thought that maybe...No—nevermind."

"No, go on." Amelia didn't want to hear it. But she had to.

"I guess, for like a split second, I had this thought today. You know, while I was with the Casters. We were just sailing through the air and I could hardly breathe and for the first time I got that rush that I feel when I'm around magic, except I wasn't scared. It's like all this time we've been using magic because we needed to, fighting because we had to survive, but when I was doing that I was just doing it because I *could*.

And the people there, they looked at me like I was...like I was impressive and interesting and..."

"I think you're impressive and interesting."

"Well, yeah. I know." Sam seemed to search her face. "I shouldn't have said anything. This was stupid. Ignore me, I—"

"No, it's not."

"It is." She began to back away. Amelia, without thinking, reached for her and took her hand under water, causing her to stop again.

It pained Amelia to get the words out, but she forced them through. "You're thinking of becoming a Caster."

"I've been thinking of becoming a Caster since I learned the word."

"No, like, one of them—rather than one of us."

Sam's eyes had gone wide like two perfectly round chestnut crystals. "Amelia," she said, "I'm not a witch."

Amelia's grip on her hand had gotten tighter without her realizing it. "I know. I know that."

"So then doesn't it kind of make sense?"

Amelia forced herself to shrug. "We've never done what makes sense. I just...want you to be happy."

"I am happy."

There was something holding Sam back, but whether it was uncertainty within or she was only feigning reluctance to spare Amelia's feelings—it wasn't clear. Amelia thought of Oscar and what Roni had told her in the café. She looked for some kind of sign in Sam's expression.

Did she like him, too? Could he have had a role in this?

And if he had...what could she do?

Her grip weakened on Sam's hand. A heavy weight had settled onto her. "You don't have to stay for me. You shouldn't feel bad just because you were afraid of hurting *my* feelings."

She had to rip the words from her throat, willing her mouth to make the right shapes, a sickly taste lining her tongue.

How could she have been so blind? All the effort they had gone to so that Sam could come here with them, all the loss that had followed for their cause, and she wasn't happy anyway. Perhaps Amelia had been too preoccupied with her own feelings to see the signs. If she had paid more attention, maybe she would have seen that Sam wasn't like the rest of them, that she was falling behind, or that she liked *Oscar* of all people. Was it that she liked him more than her?

Sam opened her mouth again, but was apparently at a loss for words. Her eyes were still wide, as if expectant. What did she want? Did she not believe her? What more was she expecting her to say?

Then Sam turned away and swam towards the pool ladder. And she was as gone as quickly as she had come, not looking back once before disappearing back inside. They had both said what they meant, but Amelia still had the distinct feeling that there was something else she didn't know.

Something Strange

Amelia wasn't sure what it was, but from the moment Elena had returned home, something was off. It wasn't her raincoat strewn over the stair rail, dripping over the carpet, or her muddy boots left in the middle of the hall. (That sort of carelessness was hardly unusual for their mentor.) It was the tone of her voice as she called out Amelia's name, a strange rehearsed quality to it.

"I'm in the study," Amelia called back. She was resting in a comfy chair with her knees to her chest, a book in one hand and Percy, her cat, curled against her side. The rain still pattered at the window beside her.

Elena appeared at the door, wiping wet strands of hair from her face. "Good, I was hoping to catch you before lunch. Where are the others?"

"Sofia and Sam went to the café to study. I think Harry's upstairs."

"Everything went alright while I was gone, then?"

Amelia nodded. "Sofi's spider got out again."

Elena smiled faintly. "Of course it did."

A beat of silence followed, longer than it should've been. Elena looked like she wanted to say more. Then didn't.

"I'll clean up, then," she said instead, already turning away. "Long day."

As she disappeared up the stairs, Amelia closed her book. She sat still in the study for several minutes, listening to the floor creak overhead, to the distant splash of running water.

By the time the rain had stopped, midday heat had begun to trickle in through the window and Elena hadn't come back downstairs. Amelia toasted herself a bagel just to have something to do with her hands.

Halfway to her room with the buttered treat, she paused near the stairwell.

There were voices, too faint to be understood. Had Sofia and Sam gotten home and she just hadn't heard them? She leaned in closer. One of them was distinctly Elena's, but she couldn't quite make out the other. If it were Harry it would certainly be louder.

Though she strained, she couldn't make anything else out. The butter was dripping down her fingers.

What am I doing? she thought suddenly. *Trying to sneak around and eavesdrop?* She shook her head and laughed inwardly at herself before simply knocking gently on the door. If they had a visitor, surely it was only polite to say hello.

Silence followed her knock, and then Elena said through the muffled wood, "Come in!"

Amelia opened the door.

No one was there. Only Elena, sitting in her chair as she weaved together a talisman. Amelia was hit with uncertainty.

"Oh. I, um..."

"Yes?" Elena continued to weave. There it was again, that practiced casual hum. If anything, the weirdest thing about Elena right then was how *normal* she was being.

"I thought I heard something."

Elena stood and set the talisman down. "I've been casting a couple charms in here, maybe that is what you heard, *cariño*." With that, she gave Amelia a quick kiss on her head and left the room.

Amelia looked around, her jaw slightly ajar. She could have *sworn* she heard her speaking with someone. Elena was odd, but not odd enough to be having a full-on hushed conversation alone in her room, replying to herself and everything.

Wait. *Replying to herself?*

She looked back to make sure that Elena wasn't going to return and then faced the room again. She thought of what she had done the night before at the pool, focusing all her energy into that one tiny point, like how a magnifying glass refracts light until it burns.

She closed the door behind her and then opened the window so that a breeze wafted its way in. The curtains flickered in the air. Good, she needed something to be moving for what she was about to do.

Summoning the magic to the surface was old news. Casting a spell was easy. What was hard for her now was keeping it contained, getting it to do exactly what she wanted. She closed her eyes and let herself feel the room around her, letting her magic bounce over every surface.

She didn't even need to open her eyes to be able to tell that time had stopped. She could feel it. She opened her eyes. Sure enough, the curtains had stopped fluttering.

Memories of Melilla flooded her mind. It felt like years ago that they had encountered Victoria on their way through the moon-cast city. But Victoria had done something then, something that Amelia had played out a few times in her head. She had manipulated time, but in a way that affected space, too. In order to keep them in the same place, to discombobulate them, she had warped the way the world moved around them, looping them over and over again.

There were so many possibilities to what Amelia could do, so many that she was just yearning to explore.

She slowly twisted her hands, imagining that time and space was being pulled with them, a glowing force caught between her figures.

And then a shadow of Elena walked back into the room. Not Elena herself—more like a projection. She walked backwards at an unnatural speed past Amelia, and then settled back in the chair. She weaved her talisman, her mouth moving but no words coming out.

And then someone else appeared in the room, clouded by a ball of smoke that quickly went away. It was Elena again.

No, not Elena, Amelia corrected herself for not the first time. *Isabel,* her twin sister. Once again, her mouth moved rapidly, gesticulating wildly, faster and faster until—

"You have to do what is right!" Isabel spoke in a low tone, but her words were sharp and clipped.

"You're a politician, Isa," scoffed Elena. "When did you begin to care about what is right?"

"When a corrupt witch arose from the dead to wreak havoc on my child's coven and tarnish the GMUC's name."

"And still that is what you care about! Reputation. Oh, it's always the same with you."

"I care about my *daughter.* I care about Sofi and her future. I will not allow you to disrupt her progress nor to scare her in one of the most formative moments of her life."

"You think she doesn't already have an inkling? Amelia is already having outbursts at the dinner table and she only learned of the existence of magical politics mere weeks ago! The only reason Sofi isn't doing the same is because she's not a confrontational witch, but she is *smart.* If you could see her—"

"Enough." Isabel shook her head. "This is not a matter of discussion. You will do as I say. You will not allow them to get involved in the Lake issue."

"You want me to *lie* to them."

"It is not a lie!" she exclaimed, before clearing her throat and starting anew in a low whisper. "I've told you already, we're taking measures. The machine—"

Elena rolled her eyes. "Right, the *machine*. I've seen it at the GMUC and it looks like a damn science class project."

"Watch your mouth."

"Eyes and ears everywhere, I'm sure."

Isabel's expression had twisted into something toxic, and perhaps Elena realized the argument was getting out of hand, because she sighed and spoke again.

"I'm not sure I could keep that promise even if I wanted to. You saw what the Hummingbird Coven was capable of in Melilla. The tabloids may border on far-fetched, but they got some things right."

"Oh, don't tell me that you of all people read *The Witch's Press.*"

"What those girls accomplished was more than a miracle. They have a gift. A gift that should be utilized."

Isabel went cold again, straightening her posture until her presence seemed to fill up the whole room. "You forget I outrank you."

Elena's gaze did not falter. She was silent for a beat. "No," she said finally. "I do not."

Suddenly, both witches' heads snapped in the direction of the door at the same time, as if they'd heard something.

"Go, quick," Elena whispered, but the witch was already gone. "Come in!" she called out, and then she faded from view, too.

By the time Amelia left the room, she was shaking. She wasn't sure if it was fear or frustration, nerves or anger towards Elena and her sister. All the reassurance the woman had given, reminding her time and time again that *the GMUC will handle it*, and yet...

It was all a lie. Once again, the adults had *lied* to her, and once again, they had done it in the name of protecting her. What else did she not know?

The edges of her vision were red.

Amelia was done with being protected.

To Weave a Narrative Together

November 2nd, 1988

Dear Victoria,

You'll never guess who I had tea with yester-
day morning. Emmaline Weaver. I'm sure you
recognize the name. We talked for an hour or
two, and at first it was just chit-chat—a bit
awkward, if I'm being honest—but then we re-
ally began to talk about what happened. Twelve
years and we were finally talking. In case you're
interested, she's doing quite fine. She married a
non-witch but I won't hold it against her. She
says she can't remember what it was like before,
which I suppose is for the best. She doesn't miss

the way things were. Not anymore, at least.

She asked if I'd ever heard from you or tried to reach out. I said no. You remember what a terrible liar I was, but I think she believed me. After all, nobody really knew how close we were, especially not Emmaline.

Now, I have to finish this letter quickly before I have to leave. I was going to meet a woman about adopting a puppy. Wish me luck.

Love,
Diana

Amelia brushed her fingers over the looping script as that single name echoed over and over again in her mind. *Emmaline Weaver.*

By now, she'd studied this letter dozens of times, reading between the lines, creating stories in her head of everything that could have happened to this woman, Emmaline. Here was what she knew: Something had occurred twelve years before the letter had been written, something drastic enough to have changed this woman's life completely.

A flicker of doubt crossed her mind. How much of this did she honestly want to know?

Before she had even really decided to, she found herself at Sofia and Harriet's bedroom door. She had been so absorbed in sifting through Victoria's letters that she wasn't even sure if Sofia was home yet, but she knocked anyway. When she heard a response, she opened the door.

Harriet was lying in her bed, shifting her hands back and forth as light danced in her fingers, rainbow rays flickering across the ceiling above her. Sofia was standing at the window with a pair of scissors and a spray bottle, snipping at the vines that crept into the room and spread over their bedroom wall. The plant had a mind of its own, wriggling gently under her touch and blooming a new flower at every spot she sprayed. She looked up.

"Are you alright? You look like you've seen a ghost."

"It's 'cause she's so taken aback by my wicked powers," said Harriet, the light still flashing between her palms. "Ooooh, Sofi, did you see that?"

Amelia ignored her and looked back to Sofia. She held up the letter. "I need records. Historical documents. Old newspapers. Something."

Sofia frowned. "Victoria?"

Amelia nodded. "In 1976 something happened to a woman named Emmaline Weaver. Something bad. And I think Victoria was responsible. No—I *know* it. If anyone is going to be able to figure this out and find where this woman is, it's you. Now, I know you don't exactly approve of all this, I know what Elena said, but you have to hear me out here. If we can find this woman, we can find Diana, and if we can find Diana, maybe we can *finally* put an end to—"

"Amelia."

"No, just listen to me—"

"Amelia, stop."

Reluctantly, Amelia paused, her mouth snapping closed as she looked at Sofia pleadingly.

But she didn't shush her again. Sofia turned away and set down her tools. She bent down and pulled a cardboard box out from under her bed. Inside were stacks of files and pages; what looked like nearly ancient texts, all frayed at the edges. She retrieved a folder and held it out.

Amelia's jaw dropped. "You already found them."

Sofia nodded, looking at her feet.

"Oh, **Sofi**, you're amazing." She ran forward and pulled her into a hug, nearly squishing the file in the process. Like the mature witch she was, Sofia accepted the hug with grace but was unable to contain her faint grimace.

Harriet was grinning. "I've been telling you that the good girl thing is an act. Sof, you're brilliant."

"There is no *good girl thing*," she quipped back. "Anyway, I haven't found everything, but I do know where to find the next clue."

"What did you find out?" asked Amelia.

"Too much." She pulled a paper from the folder and presented it.

SHOCK** IN LONDON: **Promising Young Witch Found POWERLESS After Mysterious Party Incident! Dark Magic Suspected!
April 14th, 1976

In the soft violet hours of dawn on April 11th, 1976, what should have been a routine morning for the sleepy streets of London turned into the subject of widespread magical alarm.

*At precisely 5:47 AM, a young and exceptionally gifted witch—Emmaline Weaver, 20, of the Oxford Institute of Advanced Spellcraft—was discovered unconscious and **magicless** on the lawn of a notorious vampire socialite's estate. The night before, the vampire, Graymoor, had hosted one of his infamous gatherings, but the soirée turned sinister when Weaver, last seen by classmates just before the clock struck mid-*

night, failed to return to the dormitories. Most believed she had left of her own volition.

They were wrong.

An hour after the final stragglers teleported home, Weaver was found collapsed on the lawn by a passerby, surrounded by a circle of scorched grass, which witnesses described as "reeking of spellfire." She was rushed to a local hospital where non-witch doctors declared her "perfectly fine."

The truth was anything but.

*Upon her discharge, Weaver discovered she could no longer perform magic. Not a spark. Not a shimmer. Not even a flicker. Her statement to the GMUC was chilling: a classmate identified as one **Victoria Lake** had approached her that night and performed what Weaver described as a "spell of deep extraction," one hauntingly similar to those outlawed by the Writ of Magical Integrity following the Codex Reforms of 1892, a spell which, as many will know, carries a rather **grim prerequisite...***

"Grim prerequisite?" Amelia read. And just before Sofia could explain, it clicked for her. Of course. It was how Victoria and Harriet and even the infamous witch Helga Dahle were able to use their dark power—once a witch took a life, they could suck the magic out of any other witch.

The article went on:

Sound familiar? It should. This is not the first time Miss Lake's name has been mentioned by this press. Known previously for her work alongside GMUC officials, notably in vanquishing the vicious sea creature which had plagued Mediterranean travelers for years prior to her arrival, Lake was once a revered figure herself, a young student witch from the United States with signs of a bright future ahead—at least, that was what we all thought. Now, this author is brought to wonder why exactly the GMUC would neglect to mention their prized pupil had such a horrendous ability.

Now, tragedy has struck and we are all forced to reevaluate the safety of our precious youth. Are we finally prepared to ask the difficult questions the GMUC has been avoiding?

—Mirabel Thorne, Senior Correspondent, The Witch's press

"This is..." Amelia was at a loss for words. It was so much worse than she'd thought. Not only had she stolen another witch's magic. She had *brutally attacked* her and robbed her of everything. Amelia's hand instinctively went to her chest, remembering how Harriet had described the feeling of having her magic begin to leave her. To have *all* of it taken away... Well, no wonder Diana had treated Emmaline as such a delicate topic.

Suddenly, something else clicked about the letter. "The sea monster." She looked up at the others. "She vanquished a *sea monster.*"

"So?" asked Harriet.

Amelia thought hard. "In Melilla that day, we saw Victoria so many times. In so many different timelines. What if there was another *her* that we missed? What if she had a different reason for being in Melilla?"

"You think we saw her when she was trying to kill a sea monster." Harriet's mouth popped open with an understanding, "Ohhhh."

"I don't think she *killed* a sea monster at all."

Sofia nodded. "I've checked other reports of the creature in '76. It matched the description of the one we encountered on Manon's ship, and there are no clear explanations of *how* exactly Victoria did it, which—unless it's all some enormous coincidence—means..."

"Victoria just sent the monster to our timeline, after she would already be dead, and then told everyone she'd killed it."

"For the glory, no doubt," said Harriet. "Sounds like people adored her at the time."

"Meanwhile she was jumping timelines and breaking dozens of witch laws," said Amelia, scoffing incredulously.

"Maybe it wasn't just for the glory," suggested Sofia. "Maybe she really was trying to protect people. After all, she *did* solve the problem—if only temporarily."

Harriet frowned. "I'm sorry, are you giving the witch who murdered our friend, almost murdered *us*, and tried to steal my magic the *benefit of the doubt?*"

Sofia sighed. "You're right. I just don't always think it's that simple."

"Well, I do." Harriet turned to Amelia. "So, now what?"

Harriet was actually asking her for direction. The casual nature with which she had done it made Amelia take a pause, and then she felt her heart warm slightly. The two witches in front of her trusted her. Despite everything, they truly trusted her. Not only that—they counted on her.

The warm feeling did not last. Another realization had just hit Amelia.

"She stole all of Emmaline's magic."

Harriet raised a brow. "Yeah, we covered that."

"No, I mean..." Amelia grappled with the idea. "The Victoria that attacked us in Melilla—that was not the magic of a witch *twice* as powerful as normal. Harriet, even *you* beat her. No offense. But the whole point of her going after me was that she was looking for a candidate to steal magic from, someone that would be the most compatible with her. So, if she hadn't yet stolen power when we fought her last...that means that she attacked Emmaline *after* that, which means..."

"The next time we see her, she'll be twice as powerful as before," Sofia finished the thought for her, but the manner with which she said it was not that of someone coming to this realization for the first time.

"You knew," Amelia said flatly.

Sofia was many things. A liar was not one of them. "I did."

"And you didn't say anything."

"I would have been betraying Elena. It would have scared you all, and then we'd feel helpless for a little while before deciding we had to do something about it ourselves, and then it would be *my* fault that we'd gone against her. It would have been my fault if any of us were hurt. I wasn't sure if I could live with that."

"But you decided you could," pointed out Harriet, looking at the box of records.

"Well," she shrugged. "This way, it's Amelia's fault. Since she brought it up first."

"Sofia!" Harriet cried in a mockingly scandalous whine.

For maybe the first time ever, a deathly mischievous smirk had crept onto the girl's face. Amelia had the urge to hug her again, but abstained.

"Well, it doesn't matter anyway, since you won't be betraying Elena," Amelia stated.

Sofia raised an eyebrow. "How so?"

"I overheard her talking with your mom this morning."

"She was *here*?"

"They were talking in secret, and Isabel was trying to convince Elena to *not* let us get involved. Elena *wants* to give us more freedom—it's your mother and the GMUC that's not letting her."

Sofia looked at her blankly for a moment. "So, I'd be betraying my mother."

Amelia shrugged.

Sofia had to do some real consideration then, looking from the box to Amelia before sighing. "Well, since it's all out in the open. I never got far enough to find an address. I don't even know if Emmaline still lives in London, but I do know the hospital she went to when the incident happened. They're bound to have her personal records there."

"Perfect," Amelia declared. "We can make a call and see what we can see."

"Oh, not the non-magic hospital. They didn't take her in since there wasn't a scratch on her. In the literal sense, at least. She went to a witch's hospital. They'll have her records."

"So, we'll call them."

"It's not really the kind of hospital you can 'call up' and ask for personal data from."

Amelia crossed her arms. "Well, if it's all the way in London…"

"Mhmm."

Harriet scoffed. "You want us to go to *London?*"

Before any of them could properly process the absolute ridiculousness of Sofia's proposition, a shadow fell over the floor, and a heavy creaking of wood sounded from the hallway.

"What?" a voice spoke.

Amelia turned to see Sam standing at the threshold, her expression blank.

"Who's going to London?" Sam asked.

The witches all shared a look that probably seemed much more guilty than any of them had intended. Amelia was the first to speak up.

"We found records. Well—Sofia found records. About Emmaline Weaver."

Sam still looked very confused. "Emmaline…who?"

"You remember," urged Amelia. "From this letter. Diana, she spoke to Emmaline Weaver and she wrote about it. Sofia used this clue, this name, to find out what happened. It's all here, look."

Sam took the folder and read through both the letter and the news article, her jaw agape. "I don't get it. You want to go all the way to London just to find out about this girl—well, woman. But why? What about Elena? What about the GMUC? Why does it even matter?"

"Because," sighed Amelia, "if we can find Emmaline, we can use her to track down Diana, the one who *wrote* these letters, the only one that really knew Victoria, who really knew what happened back then. And if we can actually speak to Diana, she can tell us how to put an end to this."

"We don't even know if she's alive," Sam protested. "If either of them are. What if they don't want to help us?"

"We won't find out if we don't try."

Sam paused. For once, Amelia was sounding more like Sam than Sam herself, and perhaps the girl was just now noticing. She waffled for a moment before venturing hesitantly.

"Well, then...where would we start?"

Harriet held up a hand. "I'm not sure this is a question of 'we'."

Sam frowned, then crossed her arms. "What are you saying?"

Harriet pointed to Amelia and Sam. "The two of you don't have the slightest idea of what it's like in the British Isles for witches. Sure an experienced Caster might be fine, but not one who hasn't even mastered magic yet."

"What do you mean, 'what it's like'?" asked Amelia.

"Harry," Sofia warned quietly. The other witch ignored her, moving to sit by the window. The light warped in her hands.

"Why do you think Manon and her sisters smuggled people into Spain?" she asked darkly. "Why do you think there are so many Brits around these parts? Witch trials still happen there, even if the non-witches don't see it. The entire island is crawling with hunters, and there's nothing Elena and her group can do about it, anyway, because of the darn sirens! As protective as Elena is, she's right about one thing. We're in a safe haven here. There's nowhere the GMUC has more power—nowhere that's safer from witch hunters and the like—than Europe. And America, if you count out Sam's dear old dad." It was clear that much of this had been sitting on her chest for a while.

"Don't you ever learn to shut up?" hissed Sam.

"I'm not saying it to be mean, you know." Harriet's gaze snapped back to them, her hand curling into a fist. "I used to live in England. My family still does, God knows why."

Suddenly, Sofia spoke, looking up from her pensive daze. "She's right."

"What?" Sam and Amelia said in unison.

"If we do go to London, it will be safer with Sam at home," Sofia went on.

Sam seemed to be at a loss for words.

Sofia went on, and the knife dug deeper. "After all, Victoria would never attack you. There's nothing you can give her."

Amelia opened her mouth, wanting to argue, but nothing came to her, no sensible argument, no contradicting point. The fact of the matter was, she simply did not know as much about the magical world as they did. All the books she had read, all the information she had consumed, and she had never really put much thought into the *politics* of witchcraft. And now that they mentioned it, there *were* an awful lot of Brits around their town, from the witches and Casters at the school to the adults that Elena spoke to from time to time over tea. She had never really ventured to consider that they were actually refugees. Amelia looked up.

"Maybe they're right, Sam."

Something flickered in Sam's expression, a breath escaping her. "You can't be serious."

"It's the safer option. It would be...an unnecessary risk."

She stared at her for a moment. "You mean I'd be dead weight."

"No!" Amelia cried immediately, stepping forward. "That's not what I mean. I care about you—"

"This wasn't supposed to happen." It wasn't even clear if Sam was speaking to them or to herself anymore. "All of this, the fighting, the running across the world. All of that was supposed to be over. Don't you get it? This was supposed to be our safe space." She looked at the witches around her. "This was supposed to be our happy ending. Where we finally get to *stop* and just *be*. After my d—" Her breath seemed to hitch in her chest and she could no longer go on. Tears had welled up in her eyes.

"It's not like that." Amelia reached for her hands but she pulled away. "We're not going off into battle. We're not leaving for good. We can just teleport there and back. All we want to do is talk with Diana!"

"Sure, talk with Diana." Sam wasn't looking at any of them anymore. She turned towards the door to leave. "We're going to end up just like her, anyway."

Up in a Big Smoke

The three witches left in the middle of the night, ducking behind shadows and slipping out the back door like midnight robbers. They didn't carry bags, since all of their pants pockets had been enchanted to hold infinite space a long while ago. Being the talented witches that they were and having practiced the spell they intended to use countless times before, Sofia and Harriet needed nothing but their hands. Amelia, on the other hand, was nervous as they approached the beach, water licking at her old, faded sneakers.

"Harry will go first," Sofia suggested. "That way you can watch her do it once, and then I'll be here to guide you."

"Okay. Perfect. Fine. Right." Something about the concept of being launched through time and space with nothing but the force of her own will to direct her was less than appealing to Amelia.

Harriet did as she said, bending down and placing her hand along the surface of the water, whose waves seemed to pause at her touch, as if awaiting instruction. Light rippled from her palms and she stepped into the water, still glistening with moonlight. As Amelia watched the girl walk farther and farther away from the shore, her body slowly sinking beneath the tide, she was reminded of Manon's funeral. She tried to shake the thought away, but it echoed in her mind. She recalled Sam falling to the floor in the bar that night, collapsed and helpless with a shard of glass jutting out of her shoulder. Perhaps if Sam would have already been an experienced Caster, she may have been able to deflect the blow, but in that moment, she was not like the rest of them. No wonder she wanted the fighting to end.

They had already lost Manon. She had nearly lost Sam more than once. She would not face that risk again, not in a million years.

Once Harriet was gone, a low *boom* rumbled through the ground. A flash of light rippled across the water, and then dissipated at the sand.

"Now remember," said Sofia, "Since you've never been there, it will be hard to direct yourself towards England, but focusing on Harriet should be enough. If you think hard enough about following her, your intentions and your magic will be enough to guide you. Repeat her name out loud if you have to."

Amelia nodded and then crouched before the water. She looked down at it with an accusatory frown, thinking embarrassingly, *You'd better not mess this up*, although whether she was talking to the water or herself, she wasn't sure. She steadily placed her hand atop the water's surface, and just as it had done for Harriet, it paused against her touch, waiting for her spell. She closed her eyes.

Harriet. I want to go to Harriet. She envisioned the girl's face in her mind, imagined the spell working, the light seeping from her hands before she would appear in England, rising out of the water just as the other witches had. All she needed was a little magic.

"*Aqua, portam aperi,*" she whispered. "*Aqua, portam aperi.*" It was a Latin phrase Elena had taught them, a magical incantation that they'd practiced until their tongues ached. *Water, open the gate.*

"You've done it!" Sofia called out, and when Amelia opened her eyes, she found that she had. A blue glow spread across the surface, illuminating the night for just a moment.

This was it. This was where she left Sam behind. She could do it. She was sure she could do it.

She began trudging forward and the water enveloped her. Though her T-shirt should have been sticking to her skin, it felt perfectly dry.

"Remember, think of where you want to go!" cried Sofia from behind her.

Amelia tried to think of Harriet again, but she found that the image of the girl's face was turning into something different. Although she tried, she could not shake a vision of red hair, of brown eyes rather than blue. *No,* she thought, *think of Harry. Don't think of Sam, think of Harry.*

She grit her teeth as she walked until the water came over her head and everything went pitch black.

Harry, Harry, Harry, she thought desperately.

Everything seemed to warp around her. She was moving but not of her own volition. The pitch black waters seemed to warp into something different, an erratic splash of color across her vision that spun faster and faster until she was dizzy. Something was wrong.

Harriet. Go to Harriet. Go to London.

And then it was as if something had caught on to her and she came jerking forwards. Before she could process anything, air filled her lungs and the colors disappeared.

Amelia was flung forward through time and space before landing hard on her knees. Thankfully, the ground below was quite soft and wet. Her hands sunk into the sand below her and she began coughing uncontrollably.

"Huh. You made it."

Harriet stood above her, looking down at Amelia as she crawled around desperately.

"Don't sound so—" Amelia coughed— "surprised."

Harriet shrugged. "Good on you, though."

"I think I breathed in water."

"I don't think that's possible."

Finally, Amelia was able to stand, her limbs trembling weakly. She turned and took in the moonlit city and open air before her. Everything shimmered—glass towers catching silver light like polished blades, yellow street lamps flickering in the mist like old candle flames, and the water beside her rippling with reflections that looked too strange and beautiful to be real. The air smelled like wet stone and smoke, and above it all, the low hum of London moved like a heartbeat beneath the stillness.

"Welcome to the Big Smoke," said Harriet. "It's terrible and you'll hate it. But anyway, this is the River Thames. Not sure how acquainted you are with geography—you know, with you being American and all."

Amelia shot her a look. She had, to her chagrin, not known the name of the river.

Just then, Sofia appeared out of the water, launching from the river and landing flat on the sand just as Amelia had, however, unlike Amelia, all she had to do was clear her throat before she stood.

"Amelia, you did lovely," she said all-too generously.

"Well, I've got all my fingers," Amelia pointed out thankfully just before checking to make sure she actually did.

Sofia grinned. "Perfect. Now, we just need to find our way to the hospital. If we climb up through here and get to the bridge, it should be up on the left. Just keep your eyes peeled for the Ennexus symbol." By now, it really shouldn't have surprised Amelia just how put-together and prepared Sofia managed to be. There was a sense of determination locked into her expression. One thing was true: Amelia had no qualms about following the witch into the unknown.

They did as she said and climbed up the hill of sand, but when they approached the row of vertical pillars that blocked their way, leading up to the path above, the witches paused.

"What now, oh, wise one?" taunted Harriet.

Sofia raised her arms and her green glow began pulsating around her. It was just dim enough that they hopefully wouldn't be seen, but the sight made Amelia nervous, ducking further below the bridge.

Slowly, vines began rising out of the sand, twitching and twisting their way upwards. They curled around the pillars and tightened themselves there, growing taller and taller until they reached the top. Sofia let her hands drop to her sides and a hint of a proud smile lined her lips.

"Nice one," Harriet said before promptly grabbing onto the vines and beginning to climb. The feat was easier for her than for the two other witches. Amelia, being the type to always opt for a good book on the sofa, and Sofia simply being a much slighter build, Harriet's surprising amount of muscle trumped them easily.

After the agonizing climb, the witches found themself on the empty London street, the cobblestones slick with dew. There were only a few passersby, along with rumbling cars that whipped around corners. It was true, then, that a city like this never slept. While it didn't seem like the most magical place on Earth, it was hard to believe that this place could be as dangerous as Harriet had described.

They walked down the road, staying close together. Regardless of the political climate regarding witchcraft, they were three fourteen-year-olds traveling completely alone through a strange city at night.

"Look!" Harriet hissed.

Through the blanket of darkness Amelia spotted a figure darting across the road ahead of them. No—two figures. One walked strangely with a sort of crooked limp, covered with a dark cloak down to their knees, while the other person seemed to be helping them along.

"His feet!" whispered Harriet.

Amelia squinted. There **was** something odd about the limping one's feet. They were completely different shapes. In fact, one of them appeared to be a *paw*. But why only one?

Sofia gasped beside her. "I've read about that before. Sometimes when a full moon is near, werewolves experience irregularities metamorphosing."

"I can bet where they're headed," muttered Harriet conspiratorily. "Come on. Let's follow."

And so they did. The cloaked pair took twisting turns through dark alleys, pausing every few moments.

"The change is supposed to be very painful the first couple times," Sofia whispered as they stalked along behind them.

Finally, the pair stopped before a set of marble stairs that led up to an almost monumental building, lined with strong pillars and lion statues in front of the entrance. Plastered across the front door was, as expected, the Ennexus symbol; two of the number eight, crossed over each other to make an X. Across the front of the building big letters spelled out *SAINT LAMIA PSYCHIATRIC INSTITUTE OF LONDON*.

"Why a psychiatric institute?" asked Amelia, but the answer had already come to her by the time she finished her question, a chill crawling up her spine.

"To account for the noises," replied Sofia.

The two figures limped up the stairs and disappeared through the large wooden doors, which made a booming *slam* behind them.

"And Saint Lamia?" Amelia continued.

"Lilith," Sofia provided. "You'll learn that the witches of England tend to be a bit more," she coughed, "traditional. But anyway, you can't exactly have a big sign that says 'Saint Lilith' in the middle of the city, now can you?"

Amelia looked up at the sign, tilting her head. "No, I guess not."

Sofia clapped her hands together, suddenly bearing a startling resemblance to her aunt.

"Now, we just need a plan."

Sam had never been so frustrated in her life. She sat on the sofa, staring out the window with her arms crossed as tightly as she could manage. It's not that she was expecting them to come back, but also she was *kind of* expecting them to come back. It wasn't until she heard a knock on the door that she finally let her shoulders relax. With Elena out once again on GMUC business, she had decided to take matters into her own hands.

She opened the door to find her four visitors. Adelheid, Naiara, Oscar, and Peter.

Wait—Peter?

"What are you doing here?" Sam asked him.

Naiara put her arms around his narrow shoulders with a friendly squeeze. "This is Peter. He just moved here and he's coming to our school next year! He's a werewolf, isn't that cool?"

"Um." Sam looked between Peter and Naiara. Peter shook his head ever so slightly. Of course, since the witches had never told anyone about what had happened that day on Manon's boat, it wouldn't make sense for Sam to already know Peter. "Yeah, that's cool."

"Thanks," said Peter, although she had a feeling that he was grateful for more than the compliment.

"Come in," Sam offered.

"Emily couldn't make it," explained Adelheid as she walked past. "Roni said she got sick. Or something." She winked.

Sam frowned, suddenly very confused, but the Caster girl whisked herself into the living room before explaining any further. Sam had thought they were friends with Emily. After all, Roni was her covenmate. So, what was with the wink?

As Oscar walked by, he tapped her on the head as if she were a puppy. "Ready to learn some *real* magic?"

Sam's frown deepened and she rubbed her scalp. "I thought we were just having pizza. If we blow something up in the house, Elena will kill me."

Oscar rolled his eyes and continued on. "Your loss, carrot-top."

Carrot-top?

The five of them settled into the living room and just before Sam—in the hopes of easing tension and learning more about these people who were her almost-friends—was about to ask how many of them had read the new mystery series from her favorite author, Adelheid stood and gasped. "Is that what I think it is?"

She made her way across the room to one of Elena's cabinets, encased in glass. The girl opened the door without asking and retrieved a small wooden box with swirling symbols engraved along its surface.

"It's a breaker box," she said, smiling. Oscar and Naiara voiced their interest and urged her over with the box, but Sam and Peter shared a doubtful glance.

"What's that?" asked Sam.

"It's a game," Adelheid explained. "Like truth or dare. But better. See—the box is mechanical and inscribed with runes. You set it in the middle of the table and once it activates, one of us must solve the question or challenge it gives. If you don't solve it, you get tagged on the palm. Two strikes and you're out."

Despite herself, Sam's own interest piqued. "Sounds easy enough."

"If you want to get rid of a tag," continued Adelheid, "you have to confess something personal. And it has to be an actual secret, not something made-up or something everyone already knows. If it's not a secret, the tag won't be removed."

Sam considered for a moment and then shrugged.

"Let's play."

The Game is on Again

The box game, to Sam's surprise, was actually pretty fun. They began with easy challenges, although it wasn't clear if that decision was made by Adelheid or the box itself. In fact, the tiny wooden object seemed to have a mind of its own. Once Adelheid activated it, the box began choosing players at random and presenting them with questions.

On the first turn, the box clicked, hummed, and a rune at the top glowed red. It spun towards Naiara and a compartment opened up with a tiny piece of paper, a question written on it in black ink. Naiara read the message aloud.

"Tell the group the most scandalous spell you've ever cast." She squealed in excitement. "Oh! Let me think."

After a few more turns of nothing but questions rather than challenges, Sam turned to Adelheid, confused. "So, Elena just had this thing sitting around?"

"It adapts to one's needs. The questions always depend on the person," Adelheid explained. "Although I wouldn't put it past that woman. I've heard stories about her."

Sam leaned closer. "What kind of stories?"

"Ah! Look at that, it's your turn."

And indeed, the box had turned towards Sam and began to shudder before spitting out a message. She pulled the paper out of the box and read. "*Let the person to your left cast a spell of their choice on you.*"

Sam looked to her left. Oscar sat there, looking expectant.

"I'm not sure about that," said Sam.

"Oh, come on," urged Naiara. "It's just a game!"

Sam looked back to Adelheid, who winked yet again.

Something felt wrong. Sam set down the piece of paper. "I'll sit this one out." And as soon as she said the words, a glowing red X appeared on her hand, pulsing angrily.

"First strike," said Adelheid, before taking her turn. "*Write your name on the ceiling. No ladders, no flying.* Hah! Tricky!"

The game continued on, each question seeming to rise with difficulty. They slowly moved from magic-related questions to actual challenges and dares, each one more risky than the last. Sam took it upon herself to put away the glass artifacts that Elena had left out.

As long as she didn't let herself stay still or quiet for too long, it actually wasn't so hard to distract herself from Amelia and the others' absence. (At least, if thinking about what good of a job she was doing at *not* thinking about it didn't count.)

Peter seemed to settle into the group quickly. He laughed with the others even when he tried to use Oscar's talisman to turn his own nose into a carrot and failed miserably, simply turning his nose upside down on his face for a few minutes. If Sam remembered correctly, the boy never did have the best luck when it came to changing his form. Though he was a werewolf, he was young and still couldn't change beneath the moon, a fact which remained a topic of embarrassment for him. Still, no one brought it up and he seemed perfectly content. Maybe he, too, felt a connection to Caster magic. Or maybe he simply had no one else.

It wasn't until the box settled on Sam once more that things began to go wrong. Out came the challenge, and this time Sam felt prepared as she grabbed the paper. Taking a breath, she looked down and—

Her heart dropped from her chest into her stomach. "I..." For a couple long moments, she was completely incapable of speaking. Finally, as the others watched her expectantly, she cleared her throat. "I thought these were supposed to be magic related."

"What's it say?" asked Oscar, trying to peek over her shoulder. "*Tell your best friend—*"

Sam crumpled the paper up in her fist so that none of them would see. With that, as if the box already sensed that she had no intention of following through, a second X appeared on her palm and it promptly spun away from her. She was out of the game.

She stood up abruptly. "I'm gonna get some...air." She left the room.

The sound of footsteps followed her down the hall, and when she turned to tell off whichever one of them it was, she was met with the concerned frown of Adelheid.

"Are you okay, Sam? We didn't mean to overwhelm you."

"It's not you. It's just...I don't know. None of this is right." Sam could feel her mind spiraling, and then she remembered that moment at the door and Adelheid's grim implication. "What did you mean earlier? When you winked at me?"

She seemed surprised by this. "Oh, about Emily?"

"Yeah. I thought she was your friend. Did you..." Sam leaned in close and whispered, "*poison* her?"

Adelheid snorted as if she'd said something funny. "Roni slipped something in her soup to make her sleepy. It's not like she tried to kill her."

"But why?"

"Well, don't you know?"

Sam stared at her blankly and the Caster girl laughed.

"Emily has had a crush on Oscar since primary school. She's obsessed with him."

"I kind of knew that." Sam shrugged, remembering the first day they had met and the way the girl's demeanor had instantly shifted upon his arrival—hair twirling and all. "Why should she be punished for it? She just likes someone, that's all."

Adelheid sighed, getting frustrated. "Oscar likes *you*. Roni only did it to get Emily out of the way so that she wouldn't get jealous."

A million thoughts swirled through Sam's mind at that moment, but the most prominent one was, *What the heck?*

"But...Adelheid, I don't like Oscar."

"Well, everyone thinks he's annoying at first. But trust me, he'll grow on you! We've all been talking about it and we think you should give him a chance!"

Sam shook her head, squeezing the crumpled paper tighter in her hand. Her heart was beginning to beat faster, something dangerous at the very tip of her tongue. "No, you don't get it. I—"

"I thought you said no one was home."

Sam blinked. "What do you mean?"

Adelheid was looking past her down the hall. "Hello? I don't think we've met."

Slowly, carefully, Sam turned. Behind her, standing at the very end of the hall, was a figure shadowed in black, their face just out of view. Slowly, they took a step forward, and then another, and their features seeped into the light, surrounded by light blonde curls.

The name left Sam's lips, so breathless it hardly made a sound. Nothing could be heard over the pounding of blood in her ears.

"Victoria."

"*Yes*," the witch replied, that single word laced with more venom than Sam had ever heard from another human being. Her voice had changed since she had last seen her. To Sam, she sounded older, a deeper timbre sliding off her tongue. There was something different about her eyes, too. Before, they had been a chocolate brown, much like Amelia's, something that held an almost imperceptible hint of warmth. Now, their color was almost milky—nothing but grayish emptiness within those irises.

Yes, thought Sam. She had changed.

"Did I pick a bad time?" Victoria asked, a low growl behind the sweet words. She continued moving closer. The walls seemed to shrink around her.

"*Tell me where Amelia is, Sam.*"

How did she even know her name? How had she known to come here? How could this have happened? Thousands of questions came to Sam at once, but of one thing she was certain. There was no way in hell she would betray Amelia.

For a moment, Sam felt frozen. She'd seen what Victoria was capable of, there was no way she could fight against her. But there was one thing she *could* do.

"Get out," Sam said to Adelheid. Her voice shook.

Adelheid looked confusedly from Victoria to Sam. "What's going on?" She sounded nervous now, too.

Sam pushed her back, her gaze never leaving Victoria. "Adelheid, go. You've gotta get the others out."

The Caster girl, thankfully, did not argue. She ran down the hall and Sam followed her slowly, still watching Victoria.

"You don't have to do this." Sam held out an arm. "Please."

Victoria smiled lightly as if she had said something funny. "Tell me where she is and I'll let you go."

"She's not here."

"Where is she? I won't ask again." She was only a couple steps from Sam now.

"I don't know."

A powerful force slammed against Sam and her back hit the wall. All the air and energy were yanked from her body at once. Before she knew it, Victoria was pressed against her, a hand clamped over her throat. Sam clawed at her hand, but the witch paid it no mind. Her empty, milky eyes were flashing with excitement and magic.

"I know you probably think I'm evil," Victoria said, her voice soft and falsely warm. "And that's fine. But I can show mercy. I'll leave you alone, unharmed. I only ask but one thing. *Tell me where that witch is.*"

Sam shook her head, barely able to move beneath her grip, her rapid pulse fluttering beneath Victoria's hand. She was wracking her mind for spells, enchantments, hexes, and anything that would help her—*anything* useful she had learned from those stupid classes with Elena.

Suddenly, a blast shook the house around them and Victoria went flying violently across the floor until landing at the end of the hall once more, brought down to her knees.

The Casters stood at the opposite end of the hall, Oscar at the front, and in his hand he held the small telekinetic device that most Casters carried. It pulsed with light, ready to fire again. His expression was fixated intensely on Victoria, who snarled darkly.

"That wasn't smart," she growled.

Oscar shrugged. "Never stopped me before."

Adelheid came forward and grabbed Sam, pulling her back. "Come on." Sam stumbled weakly behind her, holding her throat and coughing.

Victoria recovered quickly, rising to her feet. A cloud of black began to swirl through the air, bending around the movement of her hands as if it had a life of its own. "Casters," she muttered disdainfully.

Adelheid suddenly ripped the necklace off of her neck, and when she did, it extended in her hands, growing so long it reached the floor. In one quick motion, she tossed the chain across the five of them and tightened.

Just as Victoria's black cloud swelled and twitched, ready to attack, Adelheid breathed out a single word.

"*Abolesco.*"

The five of them vanished.

Sam only knew this because when she looked down, she couldn't see her own hands nor body. For just a moment, she wondered stupidly if she had died and was now a ghost.

Victoria paused, her cloud fading away. She couldn't see them either.

Then, Oscar spoke an incantation barely loud enough to hear. Sam wasn't sure if it was Oscar or Adelheid who grabbed her then, but she felt all of them jerk forward and into the wall, which gave out beneath their weight. Before she could process it, Sam was moving through solid concrete, now soft and malleable like water.

And then they were outside, standing next to the house in the open fields, the morning sun beating down on them. Sam looked down once more to see that they didn't even have shadows.

The others came back into view and Adelheid retrieved her necklace chain.

Peter had gone fully white. He looked at Sam. "Was that—?"

"Shhh," Naiara stopped him. She had pulled out a small jar of glittering powder and was crouching down to sprinkle it quickly over the earth. The powder left scorch marks where it touched, coming alight in bright green flame. "Hold on," she said.

And then the world fell out from underneath them.

Vision came back to Sam in spots, a sharp pain already hitting her cranium. As the world around her came back into view, she could make out Peter's face above her.

"She's awake," he said. He was holding a towel across her forehead, damp and cool. "How do you feel?"

Sam turned her head to see that the others surrounded them. Adelheid and Naiara both sat cross-legged down by Sam's feet, with Oscar pacing behind them. They all wore expressions of varying concern and worry.

"You passed out," Peter explained. Sam looked to the others with a vague sense of disbelief and they all nodded in confirmation.

Naiara spoke hesitantly. "I did a tunnel spell to bring us here and we fell through the ground, but I guess I should have warned you first. I forgot you're not familiar with magic."

Sam understood at once. Naiara had forgotten she wasn't like the rest of them. That she was different. Somehow that hurt more than the headache.

"Where are we?" Sam finally thought to ask.

"My house," Naiara replied. "We should be safe here."

Sam began to prop herself up on her elbows and the towel fell away. "We have to warn Elena. She's going to come home and she won't know—"

"Samantha," Adelheid interrupted her and wringed her hands together. "Who was that woman?"

A beat of silence passed. At first she didn't know how to answer. How could she? It wasn't something she could explain in simple terms, especially since it wasn't quite her secret to tell.

So she started with what was easy, what was true. "Her name is Victoria Lake. She's Amelia's grandmother."

No one replied at first, either from shock, confusion, or both. Peter, on the other hand, hardly reacted. He must have already known. Although he was not there that day in Melilla, he had been sitting in wait at the ship, and after all, it would have been cruel for no one to tell him what had happened to Manon—she had been a mentor to him in her own right.

It was then that she realized what she owed the Casters. She had invited them into her home, and unknowingly put them in danger. And they had saved her. With each one of their spells, they had done what she could not.

And so Sam began to tell the story. She started with the chest and the cat, which had started it all. She explained how they had all believed Victoria to be dead (which she still technically was) and how they had encountered her in Melilla. She told them what had happened to Manon and how Victoria had tried to steal Harriet's power. And then how she'd done it again with Emmaline Weaver.

"She's more powerful than ever now," said Sam. "I could see it. Something is different." She shook her head. "It's our own fault for underestimating her."

"So that's where your coven is right now?" Oscar chimed in, still pacing.

Sam nodded, warm inside. Yes, they were hers.

"You mean they went to *London?*" asked Peter.

Sam nodded again. "That's where they said Emmaline Weaver would be. Or at least where they could find her records."

"And you let them?"

"Well, there wasn't much I could do to stop them," scoffed Sam.

Peter covered his face. "This is bad."

"I don't understand." She sat up straight now. "Victoria came *here.* She doesn't know where the others are. Isn't that good?"

"Victoria or no Victoria," Oscar stepped forward, "do you have any idea what it's like in London? It's infested with witch hunters and crazed, uncontrollable magical creatures that the GMUC doesn't even have names for. It's absolute bonkers."

"He's right," Peter agreed. "It's part of why I left my pack. It's why Manon did what she did, smuggling people into Spain."

"It's why I came here with my sisters and mum, too," added Oscar.

Sam took a moment to process this. The truth was, they wouldn't be safe from Victoria either way, but if her coven was already in grave danger...

"I have to go to them," Sam stated.

"Woah." Peter held up a hand. "How hard did you hit your head?"

She shoved him in the side. "I'm serious. I should have made them take me along in the first place, but they thought it would be safe here. I thought it was better to wait than to waste my time fighting—because I was so *tired* of fighting. But the truth is..." She looked down at her hands, as if the answer could be found in her palms. "Sometimes the only way out is through."

Oscar laughed and turned away. "This girl is mad."

Adelheid and Naiara were looking at each other, their expressions very unsure. It made sense that they would not understand the gravity of the situation. Adelheid came from Germany and Naiara had been born here. Perhaps they were afraid to speak.

Peter remained unreadable for a few seconds, staring at his hands. Then, finally he said, "I'll go with you."

"What?" each person in the room said in unison.

"I'll take you to London."

Oscar scoffed. "Mate, you don't even have magic. Half an hour ago, you were sitting at the table with your nose upside down because you couldn't figure out a simple talisman."

"I might not be a Caster like you," Peter admitted, slightly flushed, "but I know London. I know how to fly under the radar and go unnoticed. When I was thirteen, I made my way out on my own, with no one to help me until I found Manon. And if I have a chance to help someone else in the way she helped me, then I'm taking it."

Sam didn't like the idea. Not at first. But something in his face told her that he had already made the decision. And besides, she didn't exactly mind having a guide.

Despite herself, she grinned.

"Then I guess we're going."

Saint Lilith

Unfortunately for the coven, the Saint Lamia Psychiatric Institute was a complete fortress. The entirety of the perimeter was surrounded by a tall concrete wall, a featureless gray mass that conveyed nothing but hopelessness. The hospital itself looked to be made of marble, monumental pillars lining its corners, with an absence of any sign of ornamentation or softness. The place must have been ancient. Amelia wasn't sure she'd ever seen anything like it. There was only one way in or out, the single set of doors at the very front, wide stone steps below them.

"Well, it has to be quite secure," explained Sofia as she wiped crumbs from her hands. They sat at a diner a couple of blocks down from the hospital. Amelia had ordered a stack of pancakes and been thoroughly disappointed when paper-thin crepes were placed in front of her. She was beginning to miss America.

"It holds the Ennexus symbol and all," Sofia continued. "Some people have caught onto its use, and so there's no way to keep it completely hidden—at least not without some very

"

advanced illusionary magic—so they protect it with practical force."

Amelia tried to salvage the crepes with a chocolate spread. "So, what you're saying is that there's no way in."

"Not exactly," Sofia clarified. "I said there's no way to get in unnoticed."

"Well we definitely don't want to be noticed," said Harriet with her mouth half full of beans. At least someone was enjoying the English cuisine, Amelia thought.

Sofia shrugged. "Or do we?"

Amelia smiled. "You have a plan, don't you?"

She shrugged again.

Harriet shook her head, chuckling softly. "It's Sofi, she's had three and half plans since we left this morning." Her eyes wandered down to the table. "Amelia, that is an obscene amount of chocolate."

"You're literally eating beans on toast."

"Up yours."

Saint Lamia was nothing like Amelia had expected on the inside. The colossal exterior was far from a disguise—nothing like the mall that resided above GMUC headquarters—but rather it was all the more grand on the inside. From the vaulted ceilings to the candelabras that floated midair, the entrance hall seemed to glitter with magic. Rows of framed portraits lined the walls, many of which looked to go all the way back to the Middle Ages. Below them, patients of varying magical race and species sat waiting in chairs. Some looked as non-magic as any other person on the street, the correct number of eyes and limbs, but Amelia caught herself staring a bit too long at the others; elfish men with greenish skin and pointy ears, stone gargoyles that grumbled and clinked heads together, and even a person covered completely in scales (and no clothes, to her discomfort). At the back of the room, speaking to the receptionist, was a man trailing along a unicorn by its reins. If Amelia weren't so nervous, she might have been a lot more excited to see a real-life unicorn just then.

As it turned out, getting inside the hospital was not the hard part. In fact, as they walked through the heavy front doors, no one gave them a second glance. One of the benefits of being fourteen; no one really cared what they did unless they were causing trouble, which they often were.

And that was when Harriet began coughing up black blood.

The receptionist speaking to the man and his unicorn caught sight of them and snapped her fingers. In response, two nurses in hooded robes materialized at the front of the room where they promptly grabbed Harriet by the shoulders and began to drag her through a door. Her covenmates followed behind hurriedly as Sofia tucked a potion back into her pocket.

As the nurses asked Harriet questions about her condition, they were led into the wards, a large room with walls chalked in runes and symbols that Amelia didn't recognize. Beds were lined up in rows, most filled with people coughing, groaning in agony, drifting into a potion-induced sleep, or all three.

"Lie here, please," the nurse instructed, her cat-like eyes glowing a sickly neon green. As Harriet obeyed, the nurse fanned out her fingers and with a flash of light, a notepad appeared in her hands. "Name, age, and coven?"

Harriet replied weakly, another droplet of tar-like blood dribbling down her mouth. She shot a look at Sofia.

However, the remorse in Sofia's expression seemed to be mostly for the nurse's sake. "We think she was hexed," she informed.

"Any past illnesses?"

Harriet opened her mouth, but began coughing uncontrollably before she could speak. Amelia caught Sofia from the corner of her eye pinching the girl's arm.

"We don't know," said Sofia. "But she's been here before? Maybe you have her records?"

The nurse nodded dutifully before scribbling it down on her notepad and handed it off to the other woman.

"Go take a look, Madge. Under Chesterfield," said the nurse.

The one named Madge whisked the notepad away and made a beeline towards a small door on the other side of the room.

"Are you sure it has to be here?" Harriet said softly enough that the nurse couldn't hear, glancing around nervously at the other sick patients. "We could go back to the waiting room..."

"You're looking better already," Sofia whispered pensively.

"Oh, that's goo—"

Sofia poured a drop from her potion bottle into the girl's mouth and quickly concealed it once more. Harriet instantly began coughing violently once more and the nurse rushed to her care.

Sofia tapped Amelia on the shoulder, but she was already on it, summoning magic to her hands.

Amelia twisted her hands, feeling as if she were bending the air and space in her grip and watched as the hurried nurses and doctors in the ward came to a pause.

Once time had frozen, Amelia ran to the door where she had seen the cloaked nurse disappear. She moved to step through and—

Gravity gave out beneath her as her foot slipped past the threshold. There was no floor on the other side, and with a gasp, she began to fall. But in a moment of quick thinking, she grasped the door frame and caught herself midair. Panting, she pulled herself back up to the ledge and looked down.

On the other side of the door was not a room, but an infinite series of floating hallways, staircases, and open doors that drifted past, moving so slowly it was nearly imperceptible. She closed her eyes and focused once more, trying to regain her grip on time, and when she opened them, the countless paths before her were completely still.

She scanned the space before her, looking desperately for the nurse she'd seen.

But instead she spotted something else. On the steps directly below, a small, black cat was sitting peacefully, swishing his tail back and forth. He was utterly impervious to the fact that time was frozen all around him.

"Oh, Percy," Amelia sighed.

As if he'd heard her, he spun around and jumped off the edge of the step and landed gracefully on the one below, then continued his gentle descent.

And then Amelia spotted the nurse she'd been searching for on a staircase a couple feet away from Percy, frozen mid-stride with the notepad clutched in her hands.

"Crap." Amelia considered her options, looking for anywhere around her that she might be able to climb down, but there was nothing in sight. "Crap," she said once more. There was no way around it.

But she was no coward. She balled her hands into fists and took a deep breath. It wasn't so far down it would hurt her (in theory) but if she missed the staircase...

Her gaze wandered further down. There was nothing but darkness, an empty abyss where the other paths faded out of view.

No. She wouldn't think about that.

She brought her hand to her chest, touching the necklace Sam had given her. The crystal hung delicately next to her heart.

Without another thought, she jumped.

The ground neared at terrifying speed, air rushing past her ears for a split second before the soles of her shoes landed on a solid surface. She wobbled precariously for a moment, leaning over the edge, and then gripped the stair railing and steadied herself, her heart pounding rapidly.

She looked forward and saw the nurse still frozen still ahead of her, facing in the opposite direction. Percy, however, was nowhere to be found. Amelia closed her eyes again and took a long, deep breath. She unclenched her hands and with that, her grip on time loosened. When she opened her eyes, the woman had already continued walking down the floating staircase, oblivious to Amelia's presence.

As the stairs moved slowly to the left, kept adrift by some invisible force, the nurse stepped off the ledge and onto a different one, where she walked through a small door. Amelia scuttled behind her and slipped through the door just before it fell closed.

The world went dark.

Something made a scraping sound, and then the room came alight once more with golden flame. The nurse was lighting the candles on the candelabra just as her eyes fell on Amelia.

With a gasp, she stopped time again. The nurse's face stayed in its shocked position, her jaw just beginning to fall.

Amelia ducked under a nearby table and time started up again.

She watched the nurse through the sheer tablecloth that shielded her. The woman was looking around confusedly, and rightly so.

Amelia held her breath.

Finally, the nurse shrugged and moved on, walking dreamily with her candelabra. Amelia sighed with relief. She continued stealthily following the (apparently not-so-bright) nurse down the hallway until they reached yet another room.

The door shut too quickly for Amelia to sneak in, so she waited in the hall for the woman to come back out, nervously looking back and forth to make sure no one came out from around the corner and caught sight of her.

Less than a minute later, the nurse returned and Amelia ducked down behind the door as she strolled off. Once the coast was clear, she slipped into the room.

When she saw the inside, she thought for a moment that perhaps this was what love felt like.

It was a library. A gigantic, gargantuan, enormous library that towered above her so high that she couldn't see where it ended. She had to squint just to see the wall opposite, which was filled to the brim with rows and rows of books. In the center of the seemingly never-ending room, there was a chandelier floating in the open air and burning purple flame. Around the candles, moths fluttered in the air. Upon closer inspection, however, she saw that they were not moths at all, but strange magical insects made of paper, small text scrawled over their wings.

A memory came to her mind. She had read about these in a page about the GMUC library. *They're lit-flies,* she thought. Tiny creatures used to navigate an abundance of records, and if her memory served her well, they could lead her to exactly what she needed.

One of the little lit-flies fluttered by her ear and she plucked it out of the air. On its back, it held a small graphite pencil which she used to scribble into its wings: *Emmaline Weaver.* Then, she sent the fly on its way and waited.

A few moments later, a file slowly floated her way, carried by a group of the lit-flies. She held out her hands and the file dropped into them. "Thank you," she said, then regretted it. She was ninety-nine percent sure the lit-fly was neither alive nor fluent in spoken English.

She looked down at the folder in her hands and sure enough, printed along the tab read *Emmaline Weaver.*

Slowly, she opened the file.

"Sofi, if you don't put that bottle away I'm going to hex your toilet again when we get home. I swear. No, stop. Look, I'm fine! I mean, not fine. I still feel plenty sick. You don't need to do that. St—!"

Harriet's complaints were silenced as Amelia appeared beside them, seemingly out of thin air. However, they knew she had simply moved very, very fast.

"I've got it, let's go!" she whispered sharply.

"We have to wait for them to discharge Harry," Sofia protested.

"Forget that." Amelia took it upon herself to loop her arms under Harriet's shoulders and yank her up out of bed. Sofia had no choice but to comply, helping her along.

Just as they were about to reach the door out of the wards, someone screeched from behind them. "Get back in your bed, witch!"

"Go-go-go-go-go," Amelia urged them through the door.

As the door began to fall closed behind them, she made the mistake of looking back.

Her breath caught in her throat.

One of the nurses was shedding her cloak, and it fell limply to the ground to reveal her feathered form below. While she had the face of a woman, her body was that of a bird of prey. She extended her wings, each one the length of a full-grown person, and dug her razor-sharp talons into the splintering wood floor. Her expression contorted into something inhuman, a wicked snarl below her beak-like snout and bright green eyes.

"*Run!*" Amelia screamed.

The girls darted through the entrance hall past the unicorn and gargoyles, past confused telepaths with white eyes, hairy werewolves, and goblin-like creatures.

There was a *BANG* behind the witches as the bird-woman came bursting out of the room, howling with unadulterated rage. Screams of terror echoed through the hall, but the coven was already pushing open the front doors, now much more heavy than they remembered.

"*Push!*" Amelia cried. "*Push!*"

With an agonizing creak, the doors opened into the sunlight, rays shining through the gap, and the witches forced themselves through until they swung open completely. But all three of them lost their footing from the momentum and the marble stairs fell out from beneath them. They each went toppling down the steps until up was down and down was up.

Finally, Amelia caught herself on one step and stopped falling. Heart pounding and breath stuttering, she looked up at the hospital doors.

The bird-woman had stopped right in front of the entrance, a couple feet above the ground, her wings flapping as she looked down on them with resentment. But she didn't make a move for them, and only let the doors fall closed until she was out of view.

Amelia sighed with exhaustion and let her head fall down to her chest. "What *was* that?"

"Harpies," Sofia coughed, her long black waves of hair falling over her face as she tried to regain her composure on all fours. "Ancient creatures often adverse to the sun, but not always and not completely. She stayed inside because she can't be seen in broad daylight." Even at her most discombobulated, Sofia was practically a walking textbook.

"She must have seen me steal this." Amelia pulled the file out from under her shirt.

"Not necessarily," Sofia countered. "They're known for their wrath."

"So I see."

"Lousy wretch," spat Harriet.

A voice spoke from behind them.

"You're not talking about me, are you?"

They all turned at once.

Sam stood there, hands on her hips with a wicked half-smirk on her face. Next to her was—to Amelia's disbelief—Peter.

"Sam?" Amelia stood on the step, looking down at the girl. The logistics of how her friend could have possibly been standing here now weren't the first thing that crossed her mind, but rather—all she could possibly be capable of thinking at that moment was how incredibly and all-consumingly happy she was that she was there.

"You're here." Amelia didn't know what else to say.

"I'm here." Sam's grin was fading, waiting expectantly for Amelia's reaction. Was she expecting her to be angry?

Amelia stepped forward and wrapped her in a hug. "I'm so glad."

But then, after that one warm moment, reality hit her once more. She pulled away. "Wait, you're *here?* How did you—? How *could* you? You said you would stay! You were safe at home!"

"I wasn't."

"Of course you—"

Peter cut in. "Your grandmother came to the house." He paused. "It feels a bit weird to call her your grandmother, doesn't it? Considering she's not even old enough to be your mother."

The other girls all nodded in agreement.

"Victoria *came to the house?*" Amelia asked incredulously. "But...why? What happened? Are you okay? Did she hurt you?" A million questions bombarded her mind at once.

"Amelia, I'm fine." Sam took her wrists in her hands. "We're fine. The Casters helped us teleport here with a few runes and some bubbles just in case, and Peter came with me to help."

Amelia blinked, her eyes catching sight of the girl's neck. "You're bruised." She grazed her fingers over the mark and Sam shuddered. She pulled her hand away and covered her mouth. It was like she had touched fire. "Oh, god."

"I'm fine," Sam repeated. "She was looking for *you.*"

Amelia didn't really care about that as much as she should have. "How did you get away?"

Sam looked over to Peter. "The Casters helped. They got us all out safe. Adelheid, Naiara, and Oscar."

"Oscar," Amelia echoed. Even the name felt wrong on her tongue.

"Yeah, who is a weirdo, by the way. Did you know that he—? Actually never mind." Sam waved a hand, looking mildly annoyed. "So, what happened in there?"

They all looked to Amelia, who felt a smile growing on her face. She held up the stolen file and they went silent.

"Emmaline is alive. And I know where to find her."

The Weaver House

Luckily for the coven and Peter, Emmaline Weaver did not actually live very far from the hospital. Unluckily for them, it was just far enough that they had to navigate the Londoner public transport system to get there.

"How about the bubbles again?" Sam suggested. "Those would get us across the city quick."

"No." Harriet would not hear another word of it.

And so it was the bus for them. After dredging up the last of their change from their pockets, convincing Sofia to transform their coins from euros to pounds, and somehow managing to get on not one but two buses moving in the complete opposite direction, they finally found what may have possibly been the right line. However, the only map they had was the combination of Harriet and Peter's foggy memory, so who knew?

"I thought you said you knew your way around London," Sam said to Peter.

"Well, when I went to France I just followed the ocean," he grumbled. "I didn't need to know street names and bus routes for that."

"What do you mean, 'follow the ocean'?" asked Harriet.

Peter tapped his nose. "Scent."

She stared at him. "You're a very strange person."

He just smiled.

When their bus arrived on the right street, the five of them rushed to get off. The driver before the driver closed them in, but weren't fast enough. The door shut on Peter's pant-leg and they all had to help him out before the bus continued on.

Amelia counted the houses as they walked down the road. "Number thirty-three, thirty-five, and... thirty-seven."

The house was bigger than she'd imagined. It was a multi-story, terraced townhouse that was sort of squished all narrow, but towered tall above them. Outside in front of the garden was a tiny mailbox, the name *Weaver* painted across it in a flowing white script.

Amelia tucked away the stolen file. All they had left to hope now was that the woman hated Victoria enough to help them, but not enough to send them away for being of her blood.

She pressed the doorbell, the ring echoing faintly from inside as the others waited with bated breath behind her. A second went by, and then another, and then another.

Finally, the door creaked open, but only a crack. The screen door still blocked them out, and so when a face appeared before them, it was too blurry to make out. A woman croaked, her head wedged through the gap in the door. "Yes?"

Amelia cleared her throat. "Are you Emmaline Weaver, ma'am?"

"Who's asking?"

"My name is Amelia. Amelia Aubert. These are my friends. We think you might be able to help us."

The woman was silent for a moment, unreadable through the screen mesh. "Help you?"

Amelia wasn't quite sure how to say it. "Victoria Lake is back."

Another beat of silence.

"And what in the ever-living hell do you want *me* to do about *that*?"

"Tell us what you know," Amelia pleaded. "Anything that can help us defeat her. And—wait!" The woman had begun to close the door. "Can you at least tell us where Diana is?"

She paused. "Diana? The witch Diana Meadows?"

"Her covenmate."

The woman laughed. "Long time since I've heard that name." She studied them all, looking Amelia up and down, and then reached forward and clicked open the screen door. But rather than invite them in, she simply left the doors open and walked away. They saw no other option but to follow her in.

She led them through the foyer to a living room with upholstered furniture and curtains lined with floral patterns and cartoonish birds. On the windowsills there were some potted plants and framed photos of vacation trips and family members. Each room smelled like old-lady perfume and cat. It was all startlingly normal.

The woman turned to face them, her face finally visible. She matched the house nearly perfectly. She wasn't as old as Amelia had thought, only in her early seventies at the most, however there was something in the way her eyes drooped with dissatisfaction, her hands trembling weakly, that gave the impression she was even older. She was about the same age as Victoria, Amelia remembered. If grandmother were still alive, this is how she would have been. She shuddered uncomfortably at the thought. Time travel was weird.

"Tea?" Emmaline asked, however she was already settling down on the sofa. "My son and grandchildren are coming over at half past, so you mustn't stay long." Her voice was squeaky and painfully English, but held the raspiness of discontent.

"That's alright." Amelia spoke for all of them.

"Then take a seat."

They did, each of them sitting on the sofa across from her, a coffee table with a burning scented candle between them; jasmine or something. Only Peter was left to stand awkwardly off to the side.

"So, you want to know about Victoria," Emmaline prompted, sighing as if she was already tired of the conversation. "Well, she was a repulsive spoiled brat when I knew her, and I was about the only one in all of London that recognized it. Proved me right in the end, though, didn't she? And if you want to know about Diana, well she was just like the rest, absolutely captivated by the concept of the girl, following her around like a damn puppy dog everywhere they went. If you ask me, I think they were having an affair before it came crumbling down that night at Graymoor's."

"The night when she attacked you," Amelia clarified.

Emmaline shot her a look. "You're a very forward little girl, aren't you?"

"I'm not a little girl."

She smiled knowingly and took a sip from her mug. "Anyway. It doesn't surprise me that Vic would come back to bite us all in the bottom now. She never did know when to stop. How did she do it, then? Time travel?"

Amelia nodded. "She died months ago. The present her. It was her younger self that came back and attacked us."

"Figures. As if a witch like that would just up and leave. Vanish off the face of the earth. Can you imagine my reaction when those buffoons at the GMUC told me she was gone for good?" She shook her head. "Nobody did their jobs back then."

"What happened that night at Graymoor's?" Sofia asked. "What *really* happened?"

Emmaline cradled her mug in her lap. "Well. It's as they say, if I'm honest. We were all partying, having a nice time, drinking, I must admit, and she and I got into a bit of a catfight. As I told you, I was the only one who really saw through her and I suppose she didn't fancy that too much. After it was all said and done, I went outside later for a smoke. She followed me. I thought she was coming back to have at it again, but before I knew it...well, she grabbed me and..." The woman frowned, seemingly unable to go on.

"She grabbed you?" Amelia urged.

"I'm not very fond of speaking about it in depth. You know the story, I'm sure. It left me...well, like this." She shrugged, showing her open hands, as if the emptiness between them were evidence for her lack of magic.

"She took your magic," Harriet supplied. This seemed to annoy Emmaline, but then Harriet continued, with an earnestness Amelia had seldom seen from her, "I know how it feels. It's awful. Like someone reaches inside of you and just pulls. But there's nothing you can do about it, and for a moment it feels like you're dying."

Emmaline had gone quiet, her eyes wide as she watched Harriet.

"I know because she tried it with me, too," said Harriet.

Whatever sympathy she'd sparked in Emmaline suddenly fizzled out. "Tried?" She laughed bitterly. "If you still have your magic, you have no idea how I feel."

"All we're looking for is a way out," Sam said softly. "We have no other options."

Emmaline sighed, looking down. "Look, girls. And, er, boy." She gestured awkwardly at Peter. "There's not much I can do for you. If you're looking for her weakness, you won't have much luck, but I can tell you this." She leaned forward. "She's hungry for power—in whatever form she can find it. Or steal it. She doesn't see when enough is enough and it blinds her. Makes her stupid. If you're dealing with the Victoria that I knew, that'll be true. She may be charismatic, and she may seem powerful, but she is weak to her core."

They all watched her intently, waiting for her to go on. Instead she picked up a notepad from the end table and began to scribble an address down in pen. "I think it's good you're going to Diana. I think she'll be able to help you more than I can." She ripped off the piece of paper and handed it to Amelia.

"Thank you." Amelia held the paper like it was treasure.

"And just to be clear." Emmaline focused more on Harriet now. "I am content with my life. I've learned to live—perhaps not like I wanted to fifty years ago, but regardless, I may not have magic but I am still free. It's been a long time since I've cast a spell. I'm not sure what kind of person I would be today if it had never happened."

She took a sip of her tea and set the cup on the table. "I wish you all the best of luck."

She stood.

"Now, get the hell out of my house."

The Wednesday Witch's Market

This time, due to some miraculous stroke of luck, the group found the correct bus going in the correct direction on the first try, and so when they all took their respective seats, they were finally able to relax for a moment. Amelia sat with Sam, Harriet sat with Peter, and Sofia sat very happily alone.

Amelia could overhear Harriet and Peter speaking in the seats in front of her.

"So, the wolf thing. It really makes your sense of smell that sensitive?" Harriet asked him.

"Yeah, I guess. More sensitive than yours."

"Right. Is that why you don't wear deodorant, then?"

Amelia decided it was probably best to ignore them, and instead focused her attention on Sam. Their shoulders brushed against each other with every rumble of the bus, but Sam was turned to the window, wordlessly watching cars pass by.

Amelia fiddled nervously with the hair tie on her wrist and looked down at Sam's hands.

Sam looked up and Amelia looked away quickly, a lump in her throat.

"So, at the witch's hospital," Sam began, breaking the silence. "What was it like? Were there, like, syringes full of beetle's blood or did they just force-feed you eye of newt?"

Amelia laughed awkwardly. She let a beat pass. "You're still mad, aren't you?"

Sam frowned. "I was never mad. I—" She took a breath. "Well, yeah. I was upset. But it wasn't like that."

"What *was* it like?"

Sam's frown deepened. "You didn't even fight to bring me." She looked away. "It was easy for you."

"None of this is easy for me."

"I mean, to leave me."

"Leaving you is never easy."

Before the silence became too heavy, Sam softened. She studied Amelia's face for a moment. "You look tired."

"Yeah, well." She didn't actually have anything else to say. She was. She had been tired for the last several weeks, and only more so as the day went on—considering she'd been busy traversing time and space while she was meant to be sleeping.

Sam watched her, wearing that expression that Amelia had seen from her so many times as of late, an expression that she still couldn't place nor understand. It was like she was waiting, constantly expecting something from Amelia—but *what?* And why wouldn't she just *say* it?

Slowly, Sam settled, her head falling gently to Amelia's shoulder, where it had rested more times than she could count. The weight was familiar and Amelia relaxed, too.

Sam brought her hand to Amelia's chest and ran her fingers over the crystal of her necklace. She whispered a spell too soft for Amelia to hear and light poured out of the crystal.

A dim image flickered in the space before them, a bluish, icy scene that Amelia had already watched a dozen times over since Sam had gifted her the necklace for her birthday.

It was the two of them together at the ice skating rink from the winter before, bundled up in puffy jackets and scarves. Sam drifted across the ice, wobbly and unsteady. Amelia stood in front of her, knees bent and still. Sam toppled over, and Amelia caught her in her arms. Then the scene faded away and the necklace was just a necklace once more.

Amelia was on the edge of sleep when a voice came from just above her.

"So, where are yous headed?"

Amelia opened her eyes.

The girl leaning on the bus seats couldn't have been older than fifteen. She had pitch black hair with bangs cut much too short. Her skin was pale and ghostly, highlighted by the dark lines drawn around her eyes and tattoos peeking out from beneath her collar, and she wore so much jewelry that she jingled as the bus moved.

Behind her, a girl and a boy stood waiting, wearing matching grins. The girl's skin was warm and dark, her face round and youthful, while the boy looked a bit older, wearing round glasses and a layered button-up. Aesthetically, none of them really fit together.

"I said, where are you witches headed?" the goth girl repeated.

Each of the witches' heads instantly snapped up to look at her.

"What are you talking ab—" Amelia began.

The girl waved a dismissive hand. "Save it." She leaned in close. "Vampires can always tell, can't they?

Amelia frowned, and then recalled the one and only vampire she'd ever been acquainted with, Gloria Grover. She had certainly been able to tell that Amelia was a witch, but how? Amelia had never thought to ask and she hadn't reached the section on vampires in her textbook yet.

"What do you want?" Harriet demanded.

The goth shrugged. "Not often we see a traveling troupe of witches and..." her gaze slid over to Peter, "werewolf?"

"He certainly smells like one," said the other girl standing further back, wrinkling her nose.

Peter sank deeper into his seat and muttered, "Why does everyone keep bringing up how I *smell?*"

"Wait, you're the vampire?" Sam suddenly asked the other girl.

The goth sneered in distaste. "Oh, you thought it was me?" She turned back to her friends and grumbled, "They always think it's me."

"It's alright, Millicent. Don't listen to them." The vampire girl rubbed her shoulder comfortingly.

"Aren't you a bit young to be immortal?" asked Harriet.

"That's actually quite rude," the vampire replied.

Harriet sat waiting for her response.

The vampire sighed. "I'm only sixteen, anyway."

"That's going to get real weird real quick."

The vampire crossed her arms defensively.

Finally the boy spoke. "Perhaps we shouldn't have come over. Have a nice day." And then the three of them were ushered away.

Amelia leaned forward to get closer to Harriet, Sofia, and Peter, itching to ask a question.

"How come the vampires can always tell?" she asked.

Sofia turned around and propped herself up on the seat to see her. "Well, so that they can turn people."

"*Turn* people? Like, turn them into vampires?"

"Effectively. Not everyone can be a vampire, you know. It's only if you already have magic in your blood. Otherwise, if a vampire bites you, all that you get is a little vertigo." One of the nice things about Sofia that Amelia would never stop appreciating was her ability to explain things without ever once taking a moment to make one feel judged for not having known it in the first place, no matter how simple the thing may be. Amelia was fairly sure that if she asked the girl how to tie shoelaces that she would instantly begin to explain the process in detail for her without a second thought.

All of the sudden, Harriet jumped up in her seat, (bumping her elbow against Peter's nose in the process, though she didn't seem to notice.) "Look!" She pointed out the window.

The others all turned to see a tiny fruit stand on the side of the road, an old man sitting idly in a foldable chair at its side.

"The dinky fruit stand?" asked Peter, still cradling his nose.

"*There.*" Harriet frantically jutted her finger.

Something small and black flashed in front of the stand, and then paused right beside it. Green eyes flashed from the tiny creature.

Although Amelia shouldn't have been surprised by now, a gasp escaped her. "Percy!"

Harriet was already jumping out of her seat, moving too fast for any of them to argue. The others could do nothing but follow. The bus was stopped at the light, so after Harriet shouted for a moment at the driver, he opened the doors for them and they all stepped off.

They all trailed behind Harriet, who was zigzagging through cars, throwing obscene hand gestures at anyone who beeped at her. But finally, they reached the sidewalk and she approached the fruit stand.

"Here, Percy, Percy," cooed Amelia, but with little success. The cat swished his tail at her with unmistakable sass. Then, he turned around the fruit stand and ducked out of sight. "Sofi, help," Amelia begged.

Sofia shook her head. "Wait a moment. He wants us to follow."

All of the sudden, Harriet gasped with realization. And yet rather than sharing her sudden epiphany with the group, she simply followed after the strange cat, disappearing behind the fruit stand.

The man running the stand was watching the five of them with nothing but mild interest.

"What the—" Amelia was caught off guard.

"Oh!" Peter seemed to realize something, and then laughed incredulously. "Oh, I remember this! It's been so long since I've been here, I didn't recognize it. Come on." And then, he, too, ducked below the stand and disappeared.

Sofia, Amelia, and Sam shared dubious glances, and then all at once shrugged and followed suit.

As Amelia went behind the stand—Sam's hand somehow having found its way into hers—the world seemed to burst into color. A cacophony of noise filled her ears, the sound of music and cheering, the smell of sugar, bread, melted butter, and perhaps hotdogs. She looked up and involuntarily stumbled forward.

It was some sort of festival or fair. The road split into three paths. The center path was occupied by a line of unicorns, ridden by people in long and intricately beaded robes who waved enthusiastically at a cheering audience. The unicorns, their horns glowing with magic, stepped to the beat of the music, moving slowly down the path as people threw cotton candy and popcorn their way.

To the right there was what looked to be carnival rides. In the distance, a ferris wheel slowly spun through the air, however the individual carriages didn't actually seem to be supported by any mechanism, but rather they floated freely through the air. Closer to them, a clown was tying up balloon animals before a crowd of squealing children. Once he finished molding together his dog-shaped balloon, he threw it up in the air and it suddenly began moving on its own, barking and licking the children's faces with a rubbery squeak.

Down the path to the left seemed to be a completely normal market—that is, if you ignored the fact that half of the vegetables set out on stands were trying to bite people.

Amelia could not suppress her wonder. "What is this place?"

"It's the Wednesday Witch's Market," said Peter. "I used to come here with my uncle. They've got everything magical you can imagine and it's all totally hidden from the public."

"Where's Percy?" asked Sam.

Sofia shook her head. "He's done his part. He can handle himself."

The five of them drifted further into the market, absorbed by wonder. Even Sofia looked mesmerized. They followed the marching unicorns, cheering with the rest of the crowd. After a little while, they were enticed by the smell of funnel cakes that permeated through the market. Sofia led them behind one of the noisy rides to summon up another handful of coins—but not before very sternly warning them all that the spell was very unethical and to only ever use it for emergencies. (They were considering the funnel cake issue an emergency. After all, they would eventually starve without food.)

The late afternoon heat intensified as the day went on. Sweat was dripping over Amelia's brow as she brushed powdered sugar off her lips. Sam walked beside her as they browsed the stalls of glittering jewels and crystals, cauldrons for sale that bubbled and steamed, glass figurines that winked at them as they walked by, and plain, unmarked boxes that were listed for thousands of pounds. The seller refused to disclose the nature of the contents.

"*We hex back! We hex back!*"

The booming chant was suddenly heard through the entire market and a crowd was forming around them, people yelling and hissing at something Amelia could not see.

"What's going on?" asked Sam, nearing the crowd and stepping on her tippy toes.

Amelia pulled her back. "Let's go." Everyone was getting closer to the crowd, trying to see *why* there was one, and in doing so simply made it bigger and made more people gravitate towards it. It was a vicious cycle she didn't want to be a part of.

Sam pulled away. "I want to see."

"No, *wait.*" Amelia reached for her again and Sam grew frustrated.

"Stop trying to control me." Her words left her lips laced in venom, but it didn't seem that was her intention, because the moment she said them, she brought her fingers to her lips.

After a moment's hesitation, Sam continued forward. Amelia looked up, and then suddenly cried out, "Sam, wait!"

Sam glanced back once more, and seemed as if she was about to argue again, but then she stopped.

Amelia was pointing up. "How about a bird's eye view?"

Sam grinned and the two girls went running in the same direction. It was one of the closed rides, some sort of tower with a fairly sturdy-looking ladder leading all the way up to the top. Amelia went first, climbing up and up, and Sam trailed close behind.

Finally, they were high enough up that they could see over the crowd. The source of the madness was a small group of green-skinned, goblin-like creatures standing in formation with cardboard signs haphazardly taped together, written with things like *EQUAL SPELLS, EQUAL RIGHTS, NO ADMINISTRATION WITHOUT REPRESENTATION*, and *POWER HOARDED IS POWER STOLEN*.

"They're protesting," said Amelia.

"Protesting what?" asked Sam from below.

Amelia frowned. She wasn't entirely sure.

Suddenly, food was flying out from the growing crowd. Popcorn, apples, and miscellaneous crumbs were being thrown at the protesters who seemed unwavering until some sort of mushy pastry landed on one goblin's face.

Three very official-looking people in black and white uniforms approached the protesters, halting the flying food with some sort of barrier spell that made all of it fall limply to the ground. Amelia and Sam weren't close enough to hear what they were saying, but they seemed to be ushering them away, covering up their signs. In response, the goblins hissed animalistically. Then, chaos ensued. People erupted into manic screams and shouts of disapproval, desperately squishing themselves in to get closer to the protesters, but were unable because of the barrier spell.

One of the people in uniform snapped their fingers and the signs in the goblins' hands vanished into thin air. They all looked rather confused for a moment, and then the official pointed a stern hand outward. With their faces twisted with frustration but their shoulders slouched in defeat, the goblins reluctantly marched away and stepped through an arch of trees in the middle of the pavement. They did not come out the other side.

Once they were gone, the crowd calmed and dispersed as if nothing had happened. The officials, too, were quickly out of sight. Amelia raised an eyebrow and passed a questioning look to Sam, who shrugged, just as clueless.

It wasn't long before the novelty wore off and the girls and Peter regrouped to find their way back out of the magical market. The sun was lowering into the city horizon, casting a golden glow across the London sights. After a few minutes' bickering, they settled on finding a hostel—a witches' hostel, of course, of which Peter and Harriet assured them there were many—and Sofia, ever the practical one of the group, revealed that she had picked up a map on the way, conveniently listing a plethora of Ennexus throughout the city.

Walking was much different from taking the bus. It was Harriet who dutifully informed them all that no one in the entire city actually had any idea how to drive, and that she was fairly sure that taking a proper driver's exam had been outlawed in London a few years back. She said this with such a grave tone that Amelia was only about fifty percent sure that she was being sarcastic.

On the bright side, Amelia was learning many new things. (Like the dozens of strange and vulgar British idioms which Harriet used on the street when a car came close to her or someone accidentally walked into her shoulder.) But there were other things, too. Being here wasn't like Elena's lessons, it wasn't like hearing second-hand about what witch culture was like. Here, they could see it, hear it, even smell the magic that wafted down alleyways.

"Oh, and one other thing," Sofia said as they walked, her neck still craned over the map. "You can't use my real name here."

"How come?" asked Amelia.

"Well, my mother is rather well-known. Moreno is a common surname but, well, just be careful."

"I had no idea your mom was that famous," said Sam, scratching her head.

"I'm not sure that's the word I'd use."

Amelia couldn't help but think back to the conversation she'd overheard in Elena's room, the pure frustration and desperation from Isabel as she demanded that Elena bend to her will. She could not imagine the responsibility that came with the woman's role, one of the thirteen most influential people in the magical world—it was an unimaginable weight.

And then she thought back to the conversation with Emmaline Weaver and the woman's characterization of Victoria. Perhaps Isabel's was exactly the kind of position that her grandmother would have killed for.

When they finally arrived at the Ennexus, they found the telltale symbol plastered over the building's door. It was listed as a hostel, however, the very walls seemed to be coming apart at the edges and the door only barely attached to its hinges.

"Is this just a facade?" asked Amelia hesitantly. "To scare away the non-witches? Like at the hospital?"

"Well, it could be!" Sofia replied rather unconvincingly. "Let's find out."

It was not. The inside was just as run-down as the outside. The ceiling above shuddered ominously and a ghostly chill ran through the air. The lobby was empty, but when Amelia really concentrated, she could have sworn she could hear whispers, but she couldn't tell where they came from.

Then, a woman came out of a tiny door with a drunken gait before situating herself behind the front desk and slipping on her glasses. "How can I help you?"

"Room for five, please," said Sofia.

"How many nights?" The woman suddenly smacked her hands together and a ball of gum appeared between them, smushed flat. She popped the gum into her mouth and began to chew.

"One." Sofia gulped.

"Right on. Here are your keys. No spell casting inside the room. That means no hexing, no cursing, no runes—it ruins the drywall—no shapeshifting of any sort, no chanting incantations, and...oh, I'm forgetting one, aren't I? Ah! That's right. No smoking."

"Thank you!" Sofia plucked the keys from the desk and the five of them began their way up the stairs.

"That'll be the thirteenth floor, dearie," the woman called after them.

A Restless Night

Amelia couldn't sleep even if she wanted to. The mattress underneath her was as hard as a rock, each individual spring poking into her spine and creaking loudly with every slightest movement. Judging by the echoing creaks from the beds around her, the others were all in the same boat. The only one that remained completely silent was Harriet, in the bunk directly above her.

Amelia was just about to reach to the side for her pants strewn on the floor and go digging through the pockets for a book when another noise made its way into the room. It was a creaking sound, but not the metal whine she had been listening to for the last several hours. This was the sound of wood straining beneath weight. Amelia did not move at first, and then she slowly shifted her position just enough to see around the end of her bunk bed. There was one singular window in the room, covered in a wrought iron grill and showcasing a view of the flat brick wall of the building opposite to the hostel. Out there, everything was silent and still.

Amelia blinked and the iron bars were gone. Simply gone.

She sat up. She could have sworn the window had been barred. And then she blinked again and she could no longer see the reflection from the glass. There was no glass on the window!

She gasped and opened her mouth to scream, and just then a hook with four points flew in through the window before being suddenly pulled back. It caught on the edge of the window, weighed down by something.

Victoria.

"Guys!" Amelia cried, getting out of bed. "*Get up!*"

In a moment of rashness and insanity, she came up to the window and grabbed hold of the hook. Using all her strength she yanked it out of where it pierced the windowpane and hurtled it back out the window. As she did, she stuck her head out and looked down.

It was not Victoria. Instead, there were about a dozen masked figures all making their way up the side of the building, climbing on their ropes hooked to each window. The one which Amelia had thrown was falling down, down, down. Attached to it was a man in all black, his face covering only pulled down half the way. He cried out in animalistic rage, limbs flailing and then—

Amelia looked away, but she still heard his body hit the ground. Bile rose up in her throat.

"What's going on?" Sam asked, her voice laced with panic. Amelia turned.

Think, think, think, she screamed internally. There were still countless of them climbing up the windows of the hostel. Even if they weren't going for their window, they only had a few moments before they would be trapped here and doomed.

And then she realized. The man had fallen. If he would have been a Caster or some other magical creature, perhaps he could have caught himself, but he had no magic of his own. His face, too, had been that of a normal human, two eyes and all. So if they weren't magic....

"Witch hunters," Amelia gasped. "There are witch hunters climbing up the walls."

"Oh, bollocks." Harriet was climbing out of bed.

Peter rubbed his eyes, his face pale with fear. "What do we do?"

All four of them stared at her with expectancy. She looked back at them with no idea where to start.

"Stop time!" suggested Sam. "Just make it stop and then bring us out of here!"

"No, they're right at the door. Even if we go back through the front door, they're probably on the stairs, blocking entrances." She balled her hands into fists. "What if I lose my grip and time starts again? It's too much of a risk, I can't control it well enough."

Amelia looked down at her hands and thought back to the day she'd overheard Isabel and Elena, how she had turned back the room and replayed the moment. True, it had been far from easy, and what she had in mind wasn't quite the same, but if she slipped up and lost her hold on it, they would still have time to get out. And that was all they needed—time.

The door rattled outside. Someone was trying to get in.

"Give me a minute," Amelia breathed, closing her eyes, trying to focus.

"They're coming," Peter said through bared teeth. The air was rising in the room, beginning to suffocate them all. Someone was shouting outside, barking orders with such a violence that a chill crept up Amelia's spine.

Elena's room had been bigger than their hostel room and she had been able to turn everything in it backwards. It was only a matter of expanding the playing field, focusing her magic on not just the room, but the entire building. And getting a stronger grip. It couldn't be that hard.

She clapped her hands together, summoning magic and energy to them and then spread them across the space before her, feeling the magic leave her body. She pushed harder and harder, letting it spread as far as it would go, and then she squeezed her hands back into fists, suffocating it.

Right there, she thought.

Though her eyes were closed, she could sense everything around her. Her magic was a part of her and everything it touched, she could feel. In that moment, she could have navigated the entire building blind.

She began twisting her hands, folding them on top of each other, pulling everything back and back and back. The difficulty grew the farther she pulled, as if the weight of the entire building was pressing down on her shoulders, her bones creaking with effort. A pained cry left her lips but she powered on. *More, I need more!*

Her grip slipped and her knees gave out. She fell to the ground, panting and coughing. She looked up.

The lights were still out. Everyone was still lying asleep. Only Amelia's bed was empty. With great effort, she shot up off the floor and peered out the window. There was still glass and there were still bars. She saw no movement on the ground below.

So she turned and immediately got to rousing her coven and Peter awake. She tapped Sofia's shoulder and shook Sam's arm. They grumbled in protest, but she yanked their blankets away and practically pushed them out of bed, whispering under her breath, *"There are witch hunters outside. Come on. Witch hunters. We have to go. Get up, Harry."*

The words *witch hunters* were what did it. They burst out of bed without another word before their clothes were (at least halfway) on. Amelia went to the door and, once ensuring the hallway was clear, they began making their way down the stairs. There was no elevator, of course. That would be too convenient.

When they reached the bottom, the lobby, too, was empty, and so was the street outside the hotel. They darted across the street and continued treading in the dark, checking around every corner.

Amelia looked back at the hotel entrance. No body. The man who she'd pushed off was nowhere to be found.

Had she really killed him? Had he even died? What if he had but she had turned back time so now it didn't matter?

Was she a murderer?

Would she have a power like Harriet and Victoria?

The thought made her ill. She ushered the others away, moving towards the light in the distance where there were more non-witches to be found. Only when they were among more people, the lingering wanderers and party-goers of the night, did Amelia finally begin to tell them what had happened.

"But what about the other people in the hostel?" Sam blurted once she'd finished.

"We couldn't have done anything," stated Amelia. "I have no idea how far back I turned time. If we would have stopped to knock on doors, the witch hunters would have come back and we would have been stuck again."

Sam shook her head, looking back towards the abandoned hostel. "We can't just abandon those people. We can go back."

"Did you even see anyone else in the hostel?" Amelia asked her.

Sam didn't answer.

"For all we know, we could have been the only ones there. I wasn't going to risk our lives for people that *might* be in danger."

Again, the others remained silent. Amelia told herself it was because they knew she was right.

"What about the hunter you pushed?" asked Harriet. "Was he dead?"

Amelia stiffened. "No, I don't think so. I turned back time before...Just before."

"How do you know?" Harriet wondered.

Amelia brushed her off. "We need to come up with a new plan. Since we don't have anywhere to stay for the night, we'll have to sleep on the bus on the way there. We can take shifts. I'll take the first, alright?"

With that, the subject was squashed and they went back to discussing their gameplan. Luckily, there were night buses that they could take to continue their way towards Diana's house in the country.

For whatever reason, they all listened to Amelia. Perhaps it was the shock from the witch hunter ordeal and they were all simply too stunned to argue, or perhaps they were all feeling so clueless that they would have accepted any sort of direction in those moments, but regardless, they listened. They took the bus and one by one took turns sleeping.

As they sat, the bus engine rumbling from beneath them, Amelia reflected on how in any other situation she might have been reeling from the power within her which she was finally beginning to master. She should have been elated at the possibility of such a thing as *time travel*, and yet whatever emotions may have risen, she was unable to feel them, unable to settle with her accomplishment or to reflect for too long.

The sun rose quickly. Amelia hardly noticed that day was creeping up on them all until light began reflecting off of Sam's hair beside her, glowing like flame as the golden sun rays made their way through the gaps in the strands. Amelia wanted to bury herself there, drinking in the light; to close her eyes and never leave again.

But that was probably the exhaustion speaking.

They switched buses and soon found themselves sailing across the long and winding roads leading into the countryside, with endless fields that stretched out like blankets across the terrain. The silence calmed her.

Then, finally, the bus disposed of them and drove away, leaving them at a stop just outside a quaint town, nothing more to be seen for miles. It was time to walk again, and so they did. They trod into the town, their legs like jelly, until arriving at a tiny house set off from the rest which matched the address Emmaline had written. There was a mailbox but it held no name.

"How do we know if this is it?" asked Peter, scratching his head.

Harriet stepped forward and opened up the mailbox. She removed a letter from inside and flipped it around, revealing that it was very plainly addressed to one Diana Meadows.

"I don't think you're supposed to do that," said Peter.

She rolled her eyes at him. "You used to illegally smuggle people for a living."

"Fair enough."

They continued forward through the garden. The plants were rather well kept, with red roses blooming on either side of the front door. When they approached, Amelia came onto the step, and then looked back and realized that none of the others had. She sighed. At least when she was older she'd be able to add "professional door-knocker" to her resumé.

And that was exactly what she did. It was rather early, and so she didn't let herself get too nervous when no response came at first. She rocked on the balls of her feet.

A minute passed. And then another. She knocked again.

What if Diana no longer lived here? What if her daughter opened the door to inform her that she'd sent her off to a retirement home? What if she had dementia and couldn't remember anything anyway? What if she was dead? What if she was secretly on Victoria's side? What if—?

The door opened.

There was no screen behind this door, and rather than only being cracked open, it swung wide and revealed the person within: an old woman, about the same age as Emmaline. She wasn't tiny like most old women, but actually considerably taller than Amelia, even though she had relaxed into a slight slouch. She had no cane, but did lean slightly on the door frame, sliding a hand into her pocket. She was a handsome woman with a squarish face. She wore a loose button-up and flared jeans with a floral design embroidered into the cuff, like someone out of a 70's magazine. Her hair was pulled into an updo, but long salt-and-pepper waves curled around her cheekbones and shoulders, framing her mildly amused expression.

"Hello, dears," she greeted, looking each one of them up and down. "How can I help you?"

"We're looking for Diana Meadows," Amelia said. She didn't really need to confirm who the woman in front of her was. She had read her letters time and time again, never having a face to attach them to, but now that she had seen her, now that she stood before her in the flesh, Amelia somehow knew. This was her grandmother's covenmate. This was Diana.

And at the same time Amelia realized it, Diana herself seemed to come to another conclusion. She studied Amelia and her eyes suddenly widened. It was like someone had slapped her across the face.

Each of them knew exactly who the other was.

"Yes," Diana said, now looking somewhat dazed. "Yes, come in."

Love, Diana

As embarrassed as Amelia felt accepting food from someone she'd hardly met, it had been hours since any of them had eaten, and so when Diana offered some bread and butter, affirmative *yes*'s left each of their mouths before they could even think.

They all sat down at her dining table on a series of mismatched chairs—since Diana was not used to this much company. They frantically ate the bread that the woman had supplied and then washed it down with hot tea, so bitter and scalding that it burned Amelia's throat, but she couldn't bring herself to care. She spooned some sugar into the tea until she could bear the bitterness and then continued on eating, only half conscious of the fact that she looked like a wild animal.

"Can I get you anything else?" Diana offered gently, her tone filled with pity.

"This is great, thanks," said Amelia, continuing to scarf down the blessedly warm bread.

After they had been eating for a little while, Diana carefully took a seat across from them all, waiting patiently for one of them to speak.

Amelia took the last sip of her tea, now practically buzzing from the caffeine, and took a steadying breath.

"So, you were Victoria's covenmate," she ventured.

It was clear Diana had seen this coming. She smiled. "I was," she replied, keeping up with the past tense. Did she even know that Victoria had died? She certainly couldn't know that she hadn't *stayed* dead.

"I don't know if you know who I am—you probably don't." Amelia picked at her nails. "My name's Amelia. I'm her granddaughter."

"I thought as much," Diana admitted. "How old are you now?"

"Fourteen." She cleared her throat and gestured to Sofia and Harriet. "So are they. My coven."

"So I see."

Amelia half expected her to ask about Sam and Peter, too, but Diana seemed perfectly content with the information given, and only waited for her to go on.

So, where did she start?

"Emmaline Weaver gave us your address." She began with what was easy and true. She explained that they had tracked her down from some old hospital records when searching for information about Victoria Lake. And then, hesitantly, she broke the news to Diana that her covenmate had passed away earlier that summer. She watched as a series of conflicting emotions passed over the woman's face all at once.

Although Amelia was fairly sure it was the woman's first time hearing the news, what passed over her expression wasn't quite as strong as shock. Her heart ached for the woman. Despite how little she really knew about their relationship, despite the hatred she felt for her grandmother, she really did regret having to tell her that the witch who she had been tied to for life since the age of thirteen was gone forever.

That is, until Amelia began to explain how Victoria wasn't really gone at all.

The mood began to change. Diana sat up straighter now and seemed to hang onto every word, and yet, once again, she didn't seem all that surprised. It was as if they were simply echoing back to her an old truth of which she had been conscious of for far longer than they had; Victoria hadn't given up the day she'd fled. She had simply changed course.

"We need to know if you can help us," Amelia pleaded. "She's after us now and she won't leave us alone until she's gotten what she wants." She searched the woman's expression desperately. "Please. You know her. You know how she works. There must be some way to stop her."

Diana shook her head, that slightly amused expression falling back into place, and she stood, facing away. "If I knew how to stop Victoria, I would have done so a long, long time ago."

"Please," Amelia begged. "You must be able to do something."

"I can hardly do anything, anymore, child." Diana reached her hand out to the table, and for a moment Amelia wasn't sure what she was doing, and then the plate in front of her began to slowly slide across the tablecloth. It stopped and stuttered before finally making its way to the other side of the table. Diana dropped her hand and drew back in on herself. "Knowledge I may be able to supply. But help? You will find no help here."

It was twice now within twenty-four hours that Amelia had come across a once-witch who had lost her magic—who had been robbed of her magic, in one sense or another. But Diana was not like Emmaline. She was not totally powerless, but rather that magic still lived within her, just out of reach. She wasn't sure which scenario was worse; to be left with nothing, or to be left with just enough that you could still hope.

"Okay," Amelia resigned. "Then tell us. Tell us what you know."

Diana sighed, looking away once more, back towards the window. "I think it would make much more sense if I were to show you."

Amelia frowned confusedly.

"Yes, I think that would be best," Diana went on, now seeming lost in thought. "Come here, little one, and give me your hand."

Amelia stood and did as she said, and the woman's wrinkled hands wrapped tightly around her own. She gazed deeply into her eyes, and suddenly a wash of calm fell over her. It was as if water was running down her body, a cool and clean mist seeping into her pores. A breath left her lungs and she relaxed completely.

Diana let her go, and the feeling began to fade, her senses slowly coming back to her

"You see," said Diana, "my natural talent revolves around emotion and the senses. Nowadays, what I just did to you is about the most I can do. However, if one of you can give me a mild boost, I believe I could illustrate my point about Vic properly."

"I can," Sofia volunteered, and offered Diana her hand. She took it gently, and then a bright green light began to seep from Sofia's skin to the woman's, illuminating her veins like a sort of bioluminescence. Diana's eyes closed with a relieved bliss. This was what she had been waiting for.

The glowing ceased. Sofia took a steadying breath, and Diana now seemed more energized. "Lovely. Thank you. Now, let's see."

She held out both hands to the five of them and they all grabbed hold of her, practically shuddering with anticipation.

The room faded to black.

Amelia wasn't sure at first where she was. There were old buildings, rowdy bars, houses with their doors open, playing music, a starry night sky hanging high above. It wasn't just an image. She could smell the ocean, feel the breeze. It was colder than she remembered, the summer heat gone. When she looked down, she found that she was wearing long sleeves and her sandals had been swapped for black leather lace-up boots.

It struck her then. She knew where she was. Melilla. But although the city triggered awful memories for her, she strangely felt no pang as she observed the city around her. No, it was not the city itself she was worried about. But she *was* worried about something. A deep anxiety was rising up in her—one she couldn't quite identify.

She heard voices nearby and her head snapped in their direction. Did she know those voices? Without making the decision to, she began walking towards where she heard them, crossing the busy street and passing in front of a brown car with an irregular sort of flat shape, its hood smooshed down and sleek.

She rounded the corner of a building and came up to a quiet alley, moonlight peering down through the cracks to illuminate the two girls standing there.

They were speaking rather heatedly. The one facing Amelia was someone she had never seen before, however, once again, she felt a sort of pull towards her. She had a severe expression, her face made of nothing but sharp angles. Her arms were crossed as she spoke to the other with a piercing venom, her voice low and raspy.

The other girl seemed to tower over the first in more ways than one. Although Amelia could not see her face, she could see her hair, a large and curly blonde puff that glistened in the blue moon's rays.

Amelia was not able to identify all of the emotions that sprang up in her just then. Her breath grew shallow as she watched the two girls speak. On the one hand, there were her personal feelings about Victoria, the spark of fear and hatred that appeared at the sight of her. But beneath that, there was something else, an emotion that was not her own, like a warm sun blossoming within her, calling her closer.

"Care to explain what that was, Vic?" the smaller girl with the sharp features asked.

A name came to Amelia's mind then. Eloise.

Victoria turned, looking around as if she had only just gotten there. She paid little mind to the other girl. "How long was I away for?"

Her covenmate's arms remained crossed over her chest, her short-cut nails tapping impatiently against brown skin. She wore a familiar judgemental frown. "You can't just disappear like that, not when we're so far from home and you know the GMUC is watching our every move."

Victoria looked up and seemed to notice something irregular. She squinted. Amelia followed her gaze and spotted a black crow perched atop one of the power lines. It blinked animatedly, flashing a deep purple glow.

Victoria sneered. "Is that...?"

"Yes, it is." Eloise sounded less than thrilled. "That entire shapeshifter family has been breathing down my neck since we reached land."

"Hmph." Victoria turned and began walking up the road where sand piled on the sidewalk. They must have been close to the beach. Eloise trailed after her, and though she didn't speak, her first question still hung in the air like a threat. "Did you need anything else?" Victoria inquired of the witch behind her.

"If you're not going to tell me, you should at least tell your *girlfriend*."

Victoria tensed and paused in the road.

She spun to face Eloise, but the witch was no longer there, having disappeared into the shadows, leaving nothing but a cloud of mist in her wake.

Amelia stepped out from behind the building, allowing herself to be seen in the light. Victoria still faced away from her, but she seemed to sense her. Amelia sensed her, too—a gentle pulsing of magic emanating from Victoria's form, drawing her near.

"Vic," said Amelia, although she was unsure of what compelled her.

The witch didn't turn, still gazing off to where Eloise had been.

"Yes, Diana?"

"Where have you been?" Amelia asked, coming around her and pushing herself into Victoria's view, demanding her attention. "Eloise has been worried sick, the GMUC sent a message, and we've all lost track of that horrible creature because you weren't where you were supposed to be. I believe we all deserve an explanation."

"Better question. Where were *you?*"

Amelia frowned in confusion.

Victoria went on. "I doubt you were with Eloise, and I *heavily* doubt that GMUC message getting straight to you was much of a coincidence."

"What are you talking about?"

"I think you were hanging around with the shapeshifters, talking with the GMUC, and telling them every little thought that came to your head."

Amelia shook her head. "What is that supposed to mean? We're here on a GMUC job. Of course I spoke with them."

"What did you tell them, Diana?" Victoria glared down at the witch, unrelenting.

Amelia didn't flinch. "Are you worried I told them about why you've been sneaking out at night? Why your your magic has gotten stronger but your control a little bit poorer? Why you're suddenly able to pull entire ships along the water like it's nothing?" She softened her voice as if they were sharing an intimate secret. "Or maybe—just maybe—you don't want them all to know that you can jump *through time* since you committed the worst crime in witch *law*."

Victoria was unable to mask her surprise.

"Yes, I know what you did, and as much as I would have liked to give you the opportunity to admit it yourself..." Amelia shrugged, but there was no question about the anger that leaked into her voice.

Victoria remained quiet for another moment, perhaps weighing her options. Finally, she returned the shrug, like she didn't know what else to do. "So?"

"So, what?"

"Did you tell them? Did you tell that vampire at headquarters?"

Amelia hesitated, conflicted. But it only lasted a moment. "No."

"No," Victoria echoed, not quite wrapping her head around the answer.

"I didn't, because as much of an absolute *idiot* you have been, I know how stupid it would be to turn you in."

Heavy silence hung between them.

"So, tell me," Amelia went on. "Where have you been all this time?"

"I took care of it."

"Of what?"

"The monster."

Amelia shook her head, not understanding.

Victoria sighed. "It's done, alright? It's gone and it's not our problem anymore."

"'Not our problem anymore'? Wha— How could you possibly have—?" Amelia suddenly paused. "No."

Victoria neither confirmed nor denied what they both knew she was thinking.

Amelia's hand raised to her lips, disbelieving. "You didn't vanquish the beast. You...you simply *sent it away.* To the future. Vic, don't you understand—?"

"I understand full well," she snapped. "This is good for us. Don't you understand? We're heroes." She studied Amelia's expression and spoke again. "Don't worry; the credit will go to all three of us. I'm not as selfish as you think I am."

Amelia was still trembling. "That's not—How could you? People will suffer for what you've done."

Victoria suddenly jumped forward, moving almost too fast to see. Grabbing Amelia by the collar, she shoved her up against the opposite wall, knocking her dizzy. "*I've* suffered. I fixed a problem for us. For all of us. You cannot imagine the lengths I've gone to—"

"Vic, have you lost all your sense?" Amelia coughed. "What are you talking about?"

Victoria's grip loosened, but she did not back away, her face so close that they were both inhaling her woody perfume.

"I can feel your magic," said Amelia, and she could. It was like the buzz that she always drew to her fingers, that low hum of power that lived within her. She could sense the same vibrations pouring off of Victoria now. And yet, it felt different. Different from *what*, she didn't know, but something felt wrong. "You feel...you're...*weaker* again."

Victoria pushed off of her, stumbling back as if she'd been slapped. Her eyes were wide and nearly manic. Amelia needed no confession—the look on her face was enough.

The words were wrenched from her chest. She bent forward, searching for any sign of remorse in the witch.

"Vic, what have you *done?*"

The Ultimate Clue

The return back to reality was not immediate. It came haltingly, as if the streets of Melilla were reluctant to fade away. First Amelia felt Diana's hand leaving hers, and then she heard the woman sigh—a painful and loaded sound. The smell of fresh bread permeated the air and finally her sight returned. Diana still sat there, looking down, her expression hidden. She did not have to wonder how she felt. It was still there, inside of her, the deep ache down to her bones, the painful strain of memories rising to the surface, the longing that had risen from the memory of Victoria's violent grip.

"That was insane," Sam blurted, breaking Amelia from her trance. "I was...*you!*"

Diana nodded. "I showed you all a memory. Unfortunately, that's all I can do."

Amelia stared down at her hands. It really was, as Sam said, insane. To live in the skin of another person, to feel their feelings, think their thoughts. It was downright surreal.

Sofia slowly raised her head to look at Diana. "The thing you said about the sea creature. Was it true?"

Diana shook her head. "I'll never know for sure. She never admitted to it."

"But you've read the news, haven't you?" she asked. "You read about the sea creature in the mediterranean that appeared out of nowhere?"

"Yes."

Amelia stood up out of her chair, not sure exactly where she was going, only that she needed to move. "She sent it to us."

Diana said nothing.

"You should have done something! You knew! We almost died that day!"

Diana just gave a slight smile. She presented her empty hands. "What could I have done?"

"You could have warned people! You knew she would come back!" Amelia began to pace across the room. "You knew she'd done something awful and you did nothing. You knew someone had stolen her magic, that she had gotten herself involved in something bad." She didn't need Diana to neither affirm nor deny any of this, because she knew it to be true. She had felt the woman's realizations in Melilla.

"I had no way of knowing exactly what she'd done that night, Amelia."

Amelia slammed her hands on the table in a moment of frustration. "So you did *nothing?*"

Suddenly, Diana stood. The table rumbled before them, an ominous vibration, a clear warning. "Enough," she said.

Amelia looked down, calming herself. "I'm sorry."

Diana's sympathetic frown returned and she sighed. "I suppose you've all had a long day."

They all nodded gravely. It was an understatement.

"I'd like to show you one more thing."

Amelia looked back up and Diana offered her hand. One by one, they all took it. Slowly, the scene around them began to shift and fade away.

Amelia's heart was pounding.

She was aware it wasn't her own. It was Diana's blood she felt pumping through her veins as she ran, dashing around corners, under glittering banners, and over rickety fruit stalls. Wind rushed through her black hair as she dove forward.

Her hands caught onto the rough fabric of someone's shirt and magic shot through her with such force that both of them jolted violently. The person she grabbed went collapsing down to the ground. She'd knocked them out, and now that they laid unconscious before her she could get a better look at the person. He was a man with a scraggly beard and dark, hollow eyes, his mouth open against the soil on the ground. Across his neck, he wore a large, silver pendant. Amelia reached into her pocket and pulled out a handkerchief, which she wrapped around her hand before grabbing hold of the pendant and breaking the clasp, throwing it to the ground.

"Diana!"

She heard the cry from above and her gaze snapped up instantly. The space around her was familiar, and it took Amelia only a moment to place it. It was the witch's market, filled with its endless rows of stalls and attractions, although the bright and joyous environment had faded away. People were running in every direction, frantic to get away, the sound of music drowned out by panicked cries. In the distance, she spotted smoke rising through the air.

Then, among the crowd she spotted a familiar face. Eloise. She was running, too, chasing after a figure shrouded in a black cloak. Amelia jumped into action, leaving the man with the pendant behind to follow after her covenmate.

"*Witch hunters!*" The desperate wails of passersby rang out through the clearing. "*Run!*"

Amelia ignored them, charging forward.

Eloise began to turn a corner where the cloaked figure had ducked behind, but just as she did, Amelia spotted something out of the corner of her eye—a woman pulling an identical cloak over her head with a grim smile.

"Eloise, *wait—*!" she began, but it was too late. As the witch turned, the woman grabbed hold of her, taking her by surprise. Within a moment, she had Eloise in a headlock, holding an iron blade a hair away from her cheek.

"Don't take another step, witch!" the cloaked woman cried, flashing a predatory grin.

Amelia stopped, holding her hands out, scanning the situation around her. What could she do?

"Where's your third, hm?" asked the hunter, her grip on the blade tightening.

Victoria. The thought penetrated Amelia's mind. Where was Victoria?

"Come out!" the woman roared into the open air. "Before I kill—!"

The word caught in her throat and her smile vanished. She seemed to be choking, trembling weakly before the blade in her hand fell to the ground. Eloise pushed away from her, free at last. The second hunter made a move towards her, but she held up her glowing hand, warning the man, and he paused.

Amelia stepped forward, squinting at the hunter as she struggled against nothing. "What...?

And then the hunter crumpled to the ground, revealing who stood behind her.

Victoria. Her skin pulsed with a deep, purple glow. She was shaking, her eyes wide with shock.

Amelia looked down to the girl's hands.

They were dripping with blood.

"Forgive me," said Diana.

Amelia blinked, adjusting once more to the change, to being back in her own skin. Diana was still in front of them, her fingers laced anxiously together.

"I know it's an upsetting scene to witness for someone of your age. But I thought it was important you had context. Not just for how Victoria became what she was, but for what she was capable of. What she was always capable of."

"That was how she got her power," said Harriet, rubbing her temples.

Diana stood and reached inside one of her cabinets off to the side. When she returned, she set a newspaper from the Witch's Press on the table before them. The headline read, ***NOVICE COVEN FOILS WITCH HUNTER TERRORIST ATTACK AT WEDNESDAY WITCH'S MARKET—AUTHORITIES LEFT SPELLBOUND.***

"This was only the beginning," said Diana. "The fame empowered her, the press only enabled her. The GMUC could never control her, and they didn't have the same measures for witches like her back then as they do today." She folded the newspaper back up as if it hurt her to look at. "It was only a matter of time before she did what she did to Emmaline."

Her words settled over the room, but all Amelia could think about was how Diana could have watched this all happen, subjecting herself to the role of the bystander. She struggled to push down the frustration that welled up within her.

Harriet's voice broke the silence. "It was me."

They both turned to her.

"In the first memory you showed us. I was the one who stole her magic that night."

Diana shook her head gently. "You know...Harriet, was it? You remind me of her, in a way."

Harriet flinched.

"I don't mean it to worry you," Diana said, an almost-laughing breath leaving her. "You all have only seen part of Victoria, but she had her virtues. She believed she could have amounted to something great, and trust me, if she would have had more patience, she could have."

"You loved her," Amelia stated bluntly. Some of her anger began to recede.

Diana paused.

"You did," Sam agreed. "I could feel it."

The woman looked down again, perhaps ashamed. But then again, this was another old truth, another thing that she had probably made peace with a long time ago. "So, I did."

"Is that why you never did anything?" Amelia asked. "Because you loved her?"

"Maybe. Or maybe I didn't love her as much as I thought."

Diana picked up the plates and cups sitting in front of them and began stacking them, wordlessly occupying her hands with the task. She took a sip of her own tea. "Now, there is one thing I can tell you all, something that may help you, something you may not know already."

"What is it?" asked Sam, leaning forward. Amelia settled back into her seat.

"There was a project on which I worked with Victoria. It was overseen by the GMUC and they paid us very generously to design it. It was a machine. A time machine, one could call it. They contracted us, overseen by a group of elite Casters, to build a mechanical device capable of replicating Victoria's abilities. They supposed that with her expertise, our coven could be an asset." She leaned forward, resting her chin on her hand. "Of course, it started out as an idea—a wild fantasy—but in her final days in London, it began to show a real promise. We were never able to finish it without her, but, Amelia," she looked her in the eye, "if your natural talent is like hers, then there is a possibility that you could finish what we worked on. The machine was meant to do more than Victoria herself could have ever dreamed of on her own. It was meant to allow one to jump through time with no magic of their own, with no consequences, with unerring accuracy. If you could find this machine, if you could complete it, you could do everything Victoria could do and more. Not only travel through decades, but do so without tiring, then fight at full strength. You could beat her at her own game and catch her off guard before she did any of the awful things that she did."

Her words hung in the air. At first, Amelia could hardly believe it. A machine that could do what Victoria did? Turning back time in one set space for a couple minutes was one thing, but to jump through *decades*... Well, that was something she had only ever imagined Victoria could do.

"How would we even find it?" she asked. "The GMUC is a fortress. They have telepaths. They'll see us coming."

Diana held up a finger. "It is difficult to enter headquarters without proper permissions, yes, but once you're already inside? Well, that's a different story. I myself have always thought that their greatest flaw was those doors which take you wherever you wish. Don't you agree?" She grinned conspiratorially.

"Once we're in, we can go anywhere we want to go," breathed Harriet in agreement.

"Indeed. You seem like a rather smart bunch. I trust you may work out the other logistics yourselves." She stood from her seat, looking down at them with earnest eyes.

"I really do hope that I have been of service. I wish you the best of luck. All of you."

They left Diana's house with a sense of hope that none of them had felt for a long while. It was unfamiliar but more than welcome.

However, whatever sliver of a plan they now had, they had to accept that it was probably not happening that day. In order to formulate a real plan, they needed somewhere to stay where they would be safe from witch hunters, goblin protesters, and shifty vampires.

Luckily enough, Harriet knew a place.

Diana's cottage wasn't far from Harriet's old home, a large and filled-to-the-brim house in an equally cramped English neighborhood where the entirety of her family lived. As they approached the house, it seemed to breathe with life. There were children's shoes and old toys scattered over the path across the garden, dirty rags hung up on the porch railing. The closer they got, the clearer Amelia could hear shouting and dogs barking from inside.

"This brings back memories," said Sofia as they stepped onto the porch.

Harriet shot her a look. From what Amelia had heard, the two of them hadn't had a very good experience when they first met either. (Something about Elena and her tendency to create a spectacle.) But it wasn't just Sofia's comment which seemed to be bothering Harriet. Her whole face was filled with dread as she rang the doorbell.

The door opened almost instantaneously, but there was no one to be found on the other side. Harriet peaked her head in and looked around. "There's no one here."

So they stepped in and began to look around.

The house itself was an eclectic mess of decorations, multicolored furniture, and tasteless wallpaper, bright and floral. The carpets were frayed at the edges and oil portraits in varying sizes and ornamentation lined the walls, each one holding an equally blonde and blue eyed family member. Amelia had to study them carefully before she finally found Harriet's, which was hidden in a corner, significantly smaller than the others, with nothing but a plain wooden frame. The girl had a grim frown in the painting—quite similar to the one she held now. But the odd thing was that while it looked rather old and faded, she looked just about the exact same as she did now, as if the painting had been done just yesterday.

"Was this recent?" asked Amelia.

"The paintings age with us," muttered Harriet, shaking her head. "Even once you're dead. That's why they keep great-great-granny's in the basement."

Amelia gulped nervously.

"MUUUUUUUUM," Harriet shouted suddenly, hands cupped over her mouth.

A plump middle-aged woman with Harriet's exact unpleasant sneer and white-blonde hair materialized at the end of the hall, a plate and teacup in hand. With a low and heavy British accent she said, "Harriet, you know how I feel about the screaming. Can't you stop it with the screaming for once? Always causing a ruckus." She tsked with annoyance and took a sip from her tea.

"Oh, yeah. Nice to see you, too, mum." Harriet's voice dripped with sarcasm. "What's up with the door?" she demanded.

The woman shrugged and waved an absentminded hand. "Well, I got tired of answering it all the time, didn't I? So I asked Nanny to whip up a mild spell so it opens on its own."

She stared at her mother. "Only for certain people though, right?"

"Sure, 'course. She also summoned up a billion quid while she was at it. And brought your great-great granny back to life. And cured cancer for everyone across the world. Y'know, just some wee basic grade-school spells." She rolled her eyes. "Really, Harriet, where do you think you are? Your great-grandmother is the only witch here besides Millie and she's older than dirt, for chrissake."

"It's *Harry*," the girl hissed. "But that just means that anyone can waltz into the house!"

"And what are they gonna do here? Hmm? Oh, you're so paranoid, aren't you? After all, we've got the dog."

"Who—Chubby?"

"'Course."

"He's a *terrier!*"

As Harriet and her mother continued bickering, Amelia shifted away in the hopes of avoiding intense discomfort. Meanwhile Peter and Sofia stayed behind, as if they thought that their presence could somehow soften the blow of the growing argument in the hall. But she had a feeling that it was neither uncommon nor likely to end any time soon. Sam was still studying the portraits.

"Who are you?"

Amelia looked down and gasped. A small child stood before her, no older than seven, holding a teddy bear in his arms. His skin was a bright lime green from head to toe. Even his hair and eyes were a vibrant foresty hue.

"Um." All things considered, it didn't take her all that long to recover. After all, she had seen much stranger things by now. "Amelia. A friend of Harry's."

"You're Harry's friend?" the child squeaked, voice rising. Slowly, his skin color was beginning to change, the green fading away into something warmer. "Any friend of Harry's..." he began, now seeming to grow taller, slowly rising up to Amelia's height as his skin and hair turned into a fiery red. He rose up and roared, "*Is an enemy of mine!*"

Amelia stumbled backwards and knocked into a table which turned out to have been holding a ceramic vase. The vase went flying down to the floor and shattered loudly before she could think to stop time.

The child—now about six feet tall and flaming red—held out his arms and from him came a booming, maniacal laugh. Just as a pair of devilish horns began to sprout from his temples, another girl stepped into the room.

"Dominic!" she cried with more annoyance than anything. She looked to be about sixteen and—judging by her pale complexion and equally light hair—was clearly another relative of Harriet's. "I told you to get my laundry, like, forever ago. What are you even doing? Don't be so annoying." She rolled her eyes and popped a bubble with the gum in her mouth.

"Hey!" the boy whined, and suddenly began to shrink back down to normal size, his skin fading into a peachy flesh-colored tone and his horns sinking back into his head. Just like that, he looked like a perfectly normal little boy, his teddy bear back in his arms, wearing a displeased pout. "You're dumb," he spat as if it was the worst thing one could say to another person.

The teen gave a half-hearted "Ugh," and walked away, never once acknowledging Amelia's presence.

Alone once more with the little boy, Amelia looked back down at him, feeling slightly calmer but all the more confused.

He wagged his tongue at her. It was forked.

"Ew," she responded.

The Chesterfields

From the moment Harriet stepped into her family home, she wanted nothing more than to get away. It started with the sight of her portrait, the smallest and least decorated of the bunch. The household had made no effort to pretend they didn't play favorites. In fact, someone who had never met any of the family could probably sort the portraits by order of most to least loved just by looking at the state of the paintings.

Then there was her mother. Harriet supposed she might not have loathed the woman so much if they didn't practically share a face. To their core, they couldn't be more different. She could not recall the last time they had been able to have a proper conversation that hadn't turned into an argument.

Her misery only deepened when she came across Dominic, determined to torment Amelia to the extent of his capabilities. He was her cousin, a shapeshifter on his mother's side, and though he had already nearly mastered his skill at his young age, he had yet to learn the most important part of being a seven-year-old boy: how to not be repulsive.

She couldn't describe the feeling that weighed upon her when she stepped into her childhood room. It was a mix between dread, disgust, and nostalgia. Either way, it wasn't pleasant. Most of the decor around the room was black. The bedsheets, band posters, the clothes hung up in the wardrobe, and even her old curtains were some shade of black or gray. There was some red, too. After all, red was the color of her magic aura, so there was no escaping it if she tried.

There were some pictures up on the wall, too, but none that she had put there. They were family photos, some framed and some strewn across the dresser. She took a closer look and realized these were the same photos that had once sat in the living room or hung up on the wall in the hallways. While she'd been gone, someone had moved them in here along with a few other useless items like the broken piano keyboard that should have gone to the basement. It seemed they had already begun to use her bedroom as storage, and it just so happened that each old photo they considered to be storage had *her* in it. From fishing trips to cousin's birthdays, each photo held her same annoyed glare somewhere among the sea of Chesterfields.

"I knew it," said a voice from behind her. Harriet turned and found her cousin, Millie, leaning on the door frame, smacking gum in her mouth while she looked the other girl up and down. "I knew you'd be back."

"It's just for the night," Harriet grumbled.

A smile crept onto Millie's face as she continued to chew. The girl had always been smug. She was the youngest of her siblings and the only one to have the witch gene activated after it had skipped her two older sisters. She had two years on Harriet, two years of continuous teasing and gloating over her talent—and then when Harriet's magic did finally manifest fully on her thirteenth birthday, it only got worse. By then, it didn't matter when Harriet, too, began to set fires without matches or cause mild earthquakes when she had a temper tantrum. She hadn't even had a third coven member, and so they all assumed she'd never mature. For Harriet, her magic was a nuisance. For Millie—whose natural talent was manipulating gravity, and so when she was younger she would simply float around the room cutely—her magic was nothing but a gift.

"Right," Millie agreed, unconvinced. She stepped over the threshold and into the room.

"Why are you even here, anyway?" Harriet asked as she got to rifling through her old things. Perhaps something here could be of use, she thought.

Millie sniffed. "My parents are going on holiday to Greece."

"So, you needed a babysitter."

She crossed her arms. "I thought I'd be so *generous* as to help out around your lousy house. I understand that may be hard for you to compute. But I could ask *you* the same thing. What happened to finding your wonderful third covenmate?"

"That's none of your business." Harriet sneered, keeping her back faced firmly towards the other girl.

Millie pouted, jutting out her bottom lip in mock sympathy. "You know, Harry, you don't have to be embarrassed. Plenty of people just don't have what it takes to be a witch."

"Don't try to bait me," Harriet snapped. "It won't work."

"Maybe my coven will let you join us. You could tag along. Like a mascot!" She popped a bubble with her gum.

Millie had always enjoyed angering Harriet. It wasn't all that hard since she was often angry with just the sight of the other girl. But she could stay calm. She had changed. Rather than snap back, she turned away without another word and began to make her bed.

Millie chuckled from behind her, as if her silence was all the more amusing. Harriet heard her footsteps trailing out of the room.

A little while later, Harriet, too, felt the need to leave her room and perhaps check to see what kind of torture her family was subjecting Peter and her coven to, but the second she stepped out into the hall, she was bombarded by some big, furry creature, baring its sharp, fangs and growling as it pounced on top of her.

"*Bruce,*" Harriet wheezed as the dog weighed down on her lungs. He began to lick her face, rolling her around on the floor.

"Oh, *Harriet*! You're home! How nice," a woman crooned from behind the dog.

With all her strength, Harriet wrenched the slobbering creature off of her and she looked up at the woman, panting.

"It's Harry."

"Right, of course," said the woman, but did not correct herself. This was her aunt Mary, Dominic's mother. She was in her late twenties, neither a witch nor a Caster, but Harriet didn't like her all that much just the same. For one thing, she had about a dozen dogs that she kept in her kennel downstairs for most of the day, and slept with all of them in her room by night, and so even when the dogs were not with her, you could smell them clearly on her clothes. "He likes you," Mary giggled as the dog nosed its way into Harriet's hair.

"Yeah, well, not as much as he likes raw meat," Harriet replied, pinching her nose to shield from the smell of the dog's breath.

"Speaking of meat," Mary began, "you'll feed them tonight for me, won't you?"

Before she could even reply, the woman clapped her hands together, looking pleased and said, "Good girl, Harriet. Thanks a lot," and strolled away.

Harriet wasn't sure how much more of this she could bear, but she continued down the hall. A distant crash sounded from somewhere upstairs and she winced. Never a dull moment.

The funny thing about the house was that no matter where you went, you always bumped into at least one other person. Whether it was midnight or afternoon, there was simply no way to pretend there was any sense of solitude. She passed by her father's office and glimpsed him reading the newspaper at his desk. Although he was a tall man (a trait which, to her chagrin, had refused to be passed down to her) he had a permanent hunch in his back from years of slouching over his work desk as he did now. His hair was a frazzled combination of silver and golden with a matching mustache that curtained over his mouth as he smacked his lips and took a sip of iced tea.

Despite herself, she lingered for just a moment outside the door, wondering if he would notice her.

He flipped a page in the newspaper, but did not look up.

She coughed.

Yet again, no reaction.

With a gentle flick of her wrist, she sent a gust of wind through the room. The air twisted and turned before taking hold of the newspaper, wrenching it out of his hands, and sending it flying out the open window. It then caught on fire before it could hit the ground below.

Her father grunted in surprise and spun to look at her.

"That draft is just awful, innit?" she said before sauntering away, quite pleased with herself.

When she reached the bottom of the stairs, Harriet came across a fight ensuing. On the one end was a five-year-old boy named Archie, (who was technically Harriet's nephew, but only because Harriet's older brother was born fifteen years before her.) And on the other end of the fight was...well, another Archie. The two boys, each with identical faces, fought over some small box, each one yanking it back in an endless game of tug-a-war.

Harriet came up to them. "Have either of you seen my friends?"

They paused, blinking up at her.

"You're not going to ask which one of us is which?" the one on the left asked.

"Don't really care, if I'm honest."

The one who had spoken frowned with dissatisfaction and then slowly his face morphed until it was Dominic who stood in front of her. He groaned frustratedly and pointed to another door. "That Sofia girl went that way."

"Cheers."

She did find Sofia in the kitchen, a very distressed strain to her face as she reached into the fruit basket on the counter.

"Everything alright?" Harriet asked.

"I just want an apple, but the fruits keep biting me."

"Oh, yeah. They do that. Here." She reached over and smacked the side of the basket and it rattled in fear. Then she plucked an apple from inside and handed it to Sofia.

"Thanks," said Sofia, though she still looked quite concerned. "Are *you* alright?"

Harriet frowned. "Why wouldn't I be?"

"It's just... your family is a bit..."

"Whatever. We won't be here for long."

"But Harry, don't you think—?"

"Think what?" Harriet snapped.

Sofia bit her lip. "If there was ever a good time to try and fix things between you and them, maybe this is it. Maybe you could all benefit from a conversation. I saw how things were when I first got here that day with Elena."

"Sofi, no offense," Harriet prefaced, "but you don't know my family."

Sofia's brow furrowed. She clearly wanted to say more, but that was the great thing about her. It wasn't just what she said that made her a good friend, but also what she didn't.

Dinner was the part Harriet always hated the most, the time of day when everyone was gathered to the long table in the dimly lit dining room to feast on a vast assortment of bland, beige food. How her grandmother could manage to give so many different dishes the same taste and texture as mashed potatoes eluded her.

"How's training then, Mills?" asked Harriet's aunt, her eyes scrunched up into an overly-enthusiastic smile as she scooped something smothered in gravy into her mouth.

"Splendid," the girl replied, though it was unclear whether she was being sarcastic or genuinely sucking up. Either way, it left an unpleasant taste in Harriet's mouth. Or maybe that was the vinegar.

"Can you believe she's already onto class C level hexes?" Her aunt chuckled pridefully to herself. "By the time we get back from Greece, she'll be streets ahead of anyone her age!"

"Very impressive," nodded Harriet's mother, with an almost wistful look in her eye. "Promising young girl you've got there, Lucille."

Harriet shot her a look which she didn't seem to notice.

"There's a hair in my food!" Dominic suddenly cried.

"Enough from you," Harriet's grandmother snapped at him.

"He just wants to start trouble, Nan," Millie told her very matter-of-factly.

At Harriet's side, her friends sat quietly, hands folded in their laps, an awkward tension settling over each of them.

"The food is very good, ma'am," said Sofia, scooping another bite into her mouth. Harriet's grandmother's reply was limited to a suspicious squint of her eyes. Sofia shared a glance with Harriet.

At the other end of the table, her uncle-in-law was attempting subtlety as he slid his plate under the table towards one of the dogs while his wife was distracted.

"Harriet," her grandmother barked, stabbing her fork into a pile of beige mush. "You're making a face."

"I'm eating," Harriet said flatly. "This is my eating face."

Millie snorted. Harriet shot her a look, and she immediately rearranged her features into a prim little smile.

"Oh, don't start," Aunt Lucille sighed at Harriet, as if she were already tired of a conversation that hadn't even happened yet. "We're trying to have a pleasant meal."

"I *am* pleasant," Harriet protested. "I'm delightful. Ask anyone who isn't related to me."

Her comment ricocheted around the table then simply dissolved into the scraping of cutlery. No answer. Not even a glare. They just... ignored her.

Harriet felt her pulse kick up irritably. Being dismissed was somehow worse than being yelled at.

"At least Millie appreciates what she's been given," her grandmother said, turning back to Aunt Lucille as though Harriet were a lamp malfunctioning in the corner. "Some young witches would kill for opportunities like hers."

"Oh yes," Harriet muttered loudly, "tragic that I'm apparently sitting around twiddling my thumbs while you heap praise on Little Miss Hex Prodigy—"

"What did I say about starting?" her aunt cut in, shaking her head. "Honestly, Harriet. Must everything be an ordeal with you?"

"It's dinner," Harriet snapped. "*It's already* an ordeal."

Sofia kicked her gently under the table, a subtle *stop before you explode* gesture. Peter stared fixedly at his plate like it might save him.

Millie tossed her hair. "Maybe if you applied yourself, you'd—"

"Oh, don't you dare give me advice," Harriet said, leaning forward. "I was brewing potions while you were still eating play dough."

"Harriet," her mother sighed, rubbing her temples. "Can't you just try to be agreeable for once?"

"I *am* agreeable! I'm extremely agreeable! No one agrees harder than I do," Harriet fired back. "You just don't like when I'm right."

Again, her words evaporated into the room, everyone choosing not to engage. Millie went back to bragging. Her aunt resumed her syrupy praises. Her grandmother complained about Dominic. It was as if Harriet's outburst had been a gust of wind hitting a brick wall: unnecessary, unnoted, and already forgotten.

"Where's Gigi?" she asked suddenly. Her great grandmother—the only other Chesterfield witch besides her and Millie—would surely understand.

"Sleeping," her mother replied curtly.

Harriet sat back in her chair, jaw tight, fingers drumming restlessly against the table.

They weren't threatened by her. They weren't intimidated by her. They didn't even dislike her.

They just didn't take her seriously.

And somehow, that was the worst insult of all.

Sofia leaned close, whispering, "I liked the part about the play dough."

Harriet huffed a short, humorless laugh.

Hurricane Harriet

After dinner, everyone began to disperse into their respective rooms, and perhaps it was because Harriet was still seething with rage, but she had forgotten one important detail: exactly where the five of them were meant to sleep. And so she had to do what any sensible girl would—berate her mother.

When she went to find her, the woman was sitting in the study, bent over a bubbling cauldron like the image of a medieval witch in a children's story.

"Mum, what are you doing?" Harriet asked as the cauldron pulsed with green glow. "Who even uses cauldrons anymore?"

"This one's electric!" her mother exclaimed, pointing to the glowing heater below it. "I told you I can be *cool.*"

Harriet sighed. "Yeah. Okay. I need to ask you where my coven's going to sleep tonight."

"Oh, well, your room should do." She continued to stir with a large wooden spoon, dropping what looked to be a dried lizard into the mix. "Do you remember when you were little and I used to brew up potions with your sister? Those were the good times, weren't they? If only your sister, Charlie, had taken up Caster magic. Couldn't handle the pressure, I always said. It's a shame when young people give up like that, isn't it?"

She had a tendency to turn every snide comment into a question, as if it softened the blow to pretend everyone agreed with her. It was one of the more irritating things about her.

"She didn't give up. She went to uni."

Her mother snorted as if she'd said something funny. "All that potential just to go to *university*. Well, I suppose if a witch never comes into her magic, there's just not much you can do. I always say, society nowadays undermines the value of a full-fledged witch, coven and all. Did you read about that elf they put on the council? Much good that'll do, I'm sure."

"Mother, *I* had no full coven for nearly a year. Not to mention, *you*—"

Before Harriet could make a point about her mother not living up to her very own standards, being a Caster herself, she was interrupted. "And I was quite worried, wasn't I? Well, at least now maybe you'll make something of yourself. Like Millie! Did she tell you that her covenmate has practically mastered water magic?"

"I'm not like Millie, mum."

"Well, no. But you could try and be a bit more like her, now couldn't you?" All of this she said without looking at Harriet once.

Harriet could contain herself for no longer. "I'd rather die."

Her mother dropped the spoon and the cauldron rattled against its metal stand. She pointed a finger at her. "That's no way to speak to your mother, Harriet."

The rattle began to intensify, not just from the cauldron, but the ground itself vibrated ever so slightly beneath her feet. "It's *Harry*."

Her mother smiled, looking at her as if she were nothing but a child who had just claimed that one plus one was five. "I named you. I think the woman who named you would know your name."

The vibration deepened, a low rumble now, but her mother still did not seem to notice.

"There's a lot you think you know," Harriet growled. "You think you know my name. You think you know the GMUC, but frankly your politics are horrid. You think you know Millie, but she's nothing but a spoiled brat. You think you know what potential is. You think you know how it should be used. But you're wrong."

Finally, her mother took note of the rumbling floor and covered her face. "Ugh. One of your tantrums again. I thought you got over this at *five*, dear," she said with a condescending smile.

The tiny electric heater below the cauldron suddenly burst into a steady flame. The potion bubbled and poured over the edge, steaming aggressively. Her mother backed away from it in haste.

"I do not have *tantrums*." Harriet balled her hands into fists. "Don't you get it? I'm doing this. I control it. And you *know* that, but you pretend to ignore it all. You pretend that you don't notice that Millie's magic is but a fraction of what mine is now, because you'd have to face the fact that you were *wrong*."

"Harriet, calm *down*."

"*IT'S HARRY!*"

The room burst into light and flames engulfed the space around them. For one moment, she could see nothing but red and orange, a blinding wave of heat and fire. She screamed, a violent cry torn from her throat, and then in one swift movement, she yanked her hands toward her chest and the flames went out just as soon as they came.

The room went silent. The fire was gone as if it had never been there at all. Nothing was charred or burned, both of them completely unharmed. The only evidence of its presence was the lingering heat that wafted through the room.

Her mother stared at her in shock, like she wasn't sure what exactly had happened. Harriet just stared back, her hands still at her chest. She trembled but not because of the magic. The magic was the least of her worries, the magic was the easiest part about what she'd just done.

And just like that, for one fleeting moment, a glimmer of understanding passed across her mother's face. It wasn't the flames or the magic which had shocked her, which had scared her. It was the speed of it all; the ease with which Harriet had pulled them back.

Harry sighed, her arms falling to her sides.

"Open a window, maybe," she said, then slowly backed away, out of sight. Her mother did not move.

She ran to the old spot at the bottom of the staircase that no one but she had ever used. The corner was shrouded in shadow. It was perfect. She collapsed there, panting, a gentle sob rising up to her throat. The flames began to creep back up on her, and though she could have silenced them, she did not. She let them swallow her, burning all around her as if she were the fiery sun itself.

Why had she ever thought it would be different? That anything would have changed in the year she'd been away?

"You don't have to do that."

Startled, she snuffed the flames out and looked up to see who had spoken. Peter stood above her, keeping his distance. She wasn't offended; after all, she had been a walking fireball only a moment ago.

"What?" she asked him.

"I'm sorry," he said. "I overheard what went on back there. I just wanted to say that the whole arguing thing, telling them what they're wrong about, trying to make them under-stand...you don't have to do it."

"And who are you to tell me what I should and shouldn't do?" she snapped back.

He held up his hands. "I just—I get it. I know what it's like."

She stood. "You don't know anything about me."

"I know how it *feels*." That made her stop so he went on, looking off into the distance like he wasn't really talking to her so much as to himself. "It feels like they just *have* to know. They have to know how they've hurt you, how they've made you feel. And it's like you convince yourself that if you can just put the right words together, say them in the right way, then you can make them *get it*. And that's all you need. But it doesn't work."

She stared at him. She was going to say something, but no words came. She settled back down onto the step.

"Should I go?" he asked, lacing his fingers together.

Silence hung for another moment, and then she said, "No."

He sank down onto the step beside her. "They're dreadful," he said.

"They're vile," she agreed.

She rested her chin on her knees. "They'll never change. Every time I think it'll be different...it's the same jokes, the same jabs. Like I'm still ten years old to them."

Peter nodded. "When I was five, I was bitten by a rogue werewolf."

She turned and looked at him, surprised.

He continued. "My parents turned me over to the pack. I guess they couldn't take care of someone like me. But the pack didn't really know what to do with me, either. You know, I wasn't born as a wolf like the rest of them and I hadn't even—" his voice cracked. He coughed, flushing. "I hadn't even turned yet. So, to my parents, I was too much of a monster. To the wolves, I was too much of a human."

Harriet knew how that felt. For a year, between having met Sofia and then finally finding Amelia, she'd lived in limbo as an almost-witch. But she'd had Sofia. Who did Peter have?

"So, to make a very long story short," he said, "I decided to run away. I was headed for France where I'd heard that magical creatures like me were protected. That's when I met Manon." He shook his head with a wistful smile. "Manon was lovely. Really. Dead smart and a born leader, but she was kind. That was the thing people always forgot. She was hard, but she did what she did because she cared." He paused and looked at Harriet. "You two are kind of similar in a way."

Harriet barked a laugh, more in surprise than anything. She had no idea how to reply. It was true that in the short time she'd known Manon, in the few times they had spoken, she'd gotten the impression that they had rested at the same wavelength, but it was the use of the word *kind* to refer to Harriet which threw her for a loop.

Peter quirked his head to the side at her and she cleared her throat awkwardly. "Go on."

"I wanted to ask you something."

She raised a suspicious brow at him. "What?"

"You don't have to answer now. In fact, you shouldn't answer now. You should think about it for a little while."

"Well, spit it out!"

"I was thinking about the day the sea monster attacked the ship and that moment when you saved me. You remember, don't you?"

She nodded, unsure of where this was going.

He fidgeted almost nervously in his lap. "That was brilliant, what you did. And I was wondering if, with everything that happened in Melilla, and with Manon gone..."

Peter stopped suddenly, his face twisting into a frown. He lost his balance on the step and fell onto his knees, his hand drawing up to his neck as he began to claw at himself like he couldn't breathe.

"Peter?" Harriet knelt down beside him, trying to get a look at his face. "Peter, what's wrong?"

His head snapped up and he flashed bright yellow eyes at her, eyes that were sharp and inhuman. He bared his teeth to reveal razor-sharp fangs dripping with drool. He growled savagely and Harriet stumbled back in shock.

He caved back in on himself, groaning in pain, and hair began to sprout from his skin, his hands turning into claws, his back hunched over and swelling. He fell forward onto all fours and in an instant, had transformed into the very image of a monster, a dark and vicious snarling creature.

A werewolf.

Harriet's gaze snapped to the open window and she threw open the curtains. A full moon shone through, its bluish light cast plainly across the werewolf. He twitched and bellowed at its touch.

The creature lunged forward without warning and Harriet, taken aback, threw her hands forward, sending a gust of wind his way that knocked him hard into the opposite wall. He crumbled and whimpered before looking up, eyes flashing with rage, and growled, a low rumble vibrating in his throat. Then, he sprung off of his back feet and ran away, so fast she could hardly process it. He darted down the hall and then was gone.

Harriet's heart pounded.

Her family was in the house. Her coven.

"*No,*" she breathed, and went running after the werewolf.

162

Seeing Double

Sam was blissfully unaware of the werewolf currently rampaging through the house.

She was busy looking for Amelia.

Although the house hadn't looked so large from the outside, it was practically a maze from within. Sam had studied a bit about space-altering charms such as the one that was cast on all their pockets to hold much more than should have been possible, and she was beginning to suspect that something similar was going on with the Chesterfield house.

She came up to a rickety staircase at the end of one hall on what she believed to be the top floor. She took each step carefully as it creaked beneath her weight. The door at the top opened easily at her push and she was suddenly exposed to the night air. She took in a deep breath, settling her nerves.

She found herself on the roof, nothing but night sky, the full moon, and the never-relenting pressure of the future hanging above her head. At the edge of the roof stood Amelia, leaning against the railing and staring out at the open fields behind the house.

"Hiding?" Sam asked her.

Amelia turned and faced Sam, a soft smile lining her lips.

"I was looking for you," said Sam. Amelia didn't respond, still smiling, so she went on. "Actually, I wanted to talk to you about something. I don't know if this is a good time, but I thought...well, that we should talk."

Amelia raised her eyebrows, waiting for her to go on.

"Right." Sam knew this wouldn't be easy. Maybe Amelia wasn't replying because she already knew what was coming. That thought didn't calm her anxiety, either.

How do I do this? How do I say this? Her heart was pounding. She had rehearsed what she had planned to say a million times over, in both her head and in front of the mirror. The same thought, the same three words had been spinning around in her head for the last month, and yet now, faced with bringing them to her lips, it was as if she had lost all knowledge of the English language completely.

"Do you remember how we met?" she asked, the words leaving her before she was even really sure where she was going with it.

Amelia nodded.

"In kindergarten," Sam went on. "Sitting on the carpet while the teacher read us a book. We were both sitting in the back and I wasn't paying attention because I was reading my own book. I remember you tapped me on the shoulder and asked what I was doing. I told you I was reading. You asked why I was doing that when the teacher was already reading us a book. I shrugged and you called me silly." She laughed, looking down at her feet. "But then you asked me what my book was about. And I told you. And then both of us stopped paying attention and we were both reading from my book instead."

She looked at Amelia, waiting for her to react, but she was still just smiling, perhaps on the edge of a laugh.

Sam took another deep breath. "I like you."

The other girl stared at her blankly and Sam realized she was going to have to be a lot more clear. That one, inconsequential word wasn't going to cut it. It didn't mean what she wanted it to mean.

"I guess, ever since all the magic stuff, it feels like things have changed." She paused. "Do you feel that?"

Once again, Amelia nodded and stepped closer.

"I don't know." Sam gulped. "I want to be...Well, I don't know what I want. I just, um. I feel differently. I feel..."

Amelia took another step closer.

Sam dropped her hands to her side. "I don't want there to be distance between us. In fact, I want...I want to be closer to you. Closer like..."

Amelia's face had broken into a wide grin. Finally she spoke. "Like you wanna...*kiss me?*"

Sam frowned and took a step back. "Your voice..."

Without warning, Amelia burst into laughter. But it was not her laugh, not the sound Sam was used to. It was almost cartoonish, wild and manic. It was the sound of a *little boy.*

"You're not Amelia," said Sam, feeling all the blood run out of her face, her body filling with dread and total humiliation. She held a hand to her mouth.

"Dominic," she choked out. "The shapeshifter."

And the little boy who looked exactly like Amelia collapsed, roaring with uncontrollable laughter.

The real Amelia was *also* blissfully unaware of the werewolf currently rampaging through the house.

She was busy looking for Sam.

It wasn't until she had come across a weak little wooden staircase at the end of the hall that she heard the sound of a voice that she recognized. With caution she climbed up said stairs until she reached the door. But she did not open it right away. Instead, she listened, pressing her ear to the thin slab of wood.

It was Sam's shaking lilt that made it through the door. "I like you."

Amelia's jaw fell open. *Who* was she talking to? She carefully turned the doorknob and peeked through the narrow gap. She could see Sam's back, but the person she was faced towards was just out of view. All Amelia could see was the edge of a shoulder.

"I guess, ever since all the magic stuff, it feels like things have changed. Do you feel that?"

Amelia tried to push the door open further but it seemed to be caught on something. Her heart was beginning to pound with anxiety. Who could it be? Certainly not one of Harriet's family members. Sam was undoubtedly spontaneous but the only other boy in the house that they'd met so far was a ten-year-old!

Could it be Peter? She blanched at the thought. Surely not, she told herself, but couldn't summon any confidence to go with the statement.

"I don't know." Sam seemed to be nearing the other person, leaning hesitantly towards them. The pit in Amelia's stomach only grew. She continued pressing her weight against the door. "I want to be...Well, I don't know what I want. I just, um. I feel differently. I feel..."

The door was beginning to give. Just a little bit more and—

The other voice finally spoke. ""Like you wanna...*kiss me?*"

Did Amelia know that voice? It sounded familiar but she couldn't put her finger on it. It sounded almost like a...*child.* But it couldn't be, could it?

"Your voice..."

There was a sudden roar of laughter.

"You're not Amelia," said Sam. "Dominic. The shapeshifter."

The door finally gave way and Amelia went flying forward. She was momentarily blinded by her frazzled curls, but once she threw them out of her face, she could finally see who Sam was speaking to.

It was *her.* Amelia herself.

"What the—?" Amelia began.

And then the world seemed to fall apart.

The figure who looked like Amelia suddenly brought his hands to his throat, his eyes widening. He began to rise up off the ground, his legs swinging desperately in the air. He choked helplessly, held up by some invisible force. Sam was backing away, fear and confusion written across her face.

"Sam, get back!" Amelia cried.

The girl's head snapped back towards her and she only looked all the more confused.

Then, another figure began to flicker into view in front of the imposter. First, a pair of feet came into view through the fog, floating midair, and then her legs, and then those all-too-familiar golden curls seemed to light up the night sky.

Victoria levitated above them all, gripping the shapeshifter by the neck. It was a ghastly sight for Amelia, watching as her own face contorted with pain. But something began to shift—the shapeshifter's curly brown hair shrank back into his head and his legs slowly shortened, his clothes turning from a plain tank top and shorts to a dinosaur T-shirt and mismatched socks. His hair turned blond and his eyes blue.

Victoria's face twisted into shock as she looked upon struggling Dominic.

Amelia knew what the witch was trying to do. And why she had failed. A witch could not steal the magic of a shapeshifter, no matter how much that shapeshifter looked like her own flesh and blood.

Amelia had hesitated before. She had let too many opportunities to put an end to this all slip out from beneath her. She would not let it happen again. She ran through dozens of Elena's lessons in her mind, racking her brain for anything useful that she'd learned, any spell that would do the damage that this witch deserved.

In that moment, she wished for Harriet's fire or her wind, for Sofia's call to the animals around her, or even for Elena's illusionary magic. But she supposed one had to work with what they were given.

Just then, a word came to her mind. She pulled back her hands, pulling magic to her fingers, and balled up every ounce of energy she had in between her palms and purple glow pulsed from her, begging to be released.

One glorious word came to mind.

"*Demolire!*" she cried.

Destroy.

She wasn't sure how much of it was the word itself or the pure rage laced into it, but when she shot her hands forward, she felt a surge like never before. Victoria barely had time to turn before the purple ball of flames crashed into her with so much force that it shook the very earth beneath them.

Amelia's teeth rattled in her head. She watched as Victoria began to crumple, smoke blurring the air around her. Surely the pure energy that had passed through Amelia had been enough to finally do the witch some real damage.

Dominic was released from her grip and fell back to the roof of the house. Sam ran to him, grabbing him by the shoulders and shaking him until he stirred again. Amelia wanted to scream at her to leave him, but she was already pulling the small boy to his feet, dragging him back.

Meanwhile, Victoria was still in the air and the smoke was dissipating. She faced Amelia now, her dark snarl slowly coming into view. All that she could think of in that moment was the story Emmaline had told, her complete loss of magic—a magic which now rested in Victoria's hands.

Amelia expected the witch to explode with rage, to instantly return the spell. For there was not a mark on her, no visible damage she could see. But instead, she drifted down slowly, her feet landing gently on the roof before she strolled toward Amelia. Though her movements looked languid and almost lazy, that rage still bubbled visibly within her. The false calm only made Amelia more nervous.

Victoria tilted her head. "I'm not going to kill you, Amelia."

She didn't respond, raising her glowing hands in anticipation. Victoria sighed at the sight of them.

"I made a mistake last time. I understand that now. I waited too long. Stalking, lingering around you and your friends."

"You don't have to do this," said Amelia. "This doesn't end well for you. I've seen it."

This seemed to amuse her. "Who are you to tell me about the future?"

The witch began to glow. Not like Amelia's glow, a slow and steady build-up to that magical shine. Her aura was purple, a deep and wicked color that seemed to burst from her instantly as if it took no effort at all—as if magic lived in the outer layers of her skin, just waiting for the slightest call to be released. It was blinding.

But before the magic could leave her, something crashed from behind Amelia and the door to the roof went flying into the air off the edge. Wood splinters prickled her skin and she shielded her eyes. A dark cloud too fast for her to make out darted across her vision. Something big. Something alive.

A deafening roar rang out through the night, the bellow of a monstrous creature, a sound that rattled her very bones. The creature slammed into Victoria, knocking her off her feet like she was nothing more than a rag doll. Shining white fangs glistened in the dark, viciously tearing into the witch.

And then Harriet was there, crawling through the rubble where the door to the house had been. "*Peter!*" she shouted. Her face was smudged with dust and soot. On her knees, she raised her hand and sent a surge of wind towards the creature, knocking both of them off balance.

Victoria wrenched herself from the monster's grip and only then could Amelia see what it really was, an image that she'd only seen in text and spellbooks, an idea she had once only read about in *storybooks*. It was a werewolf, reeling back on its bony haunches, baring its sharp teeth, lips pulled back into a bone-chilling scowl. He lunged mindlessly for Victoria, who for once seemed completely unprepared. Perhaps it was more difficult for her to anticipate the creature's blows and bites, because it seemed utterly out of control. The creature made contact and they broke through the railing along the edge of the roof. They toppled over the edge, out of sight in an instant.

Harriet cried out, and at first Amelia didn't understand why.

Peter. The wolf was Peter.

She was on her feet at once, running to where she'd seen them fall. Harriet was at her side as they both leaned over to see, but there were only the remnants of what had once been the Chesterfields' garden. Everything was in pieces, dirt flung across the entire yard with strips of vines and flowers chewed up across the ground. Up ahead, Victoria and the wolf had already made their way outside the fence, tumbling over each other in a vicious battle. They tore through the earth, going up in a cloud of dust and dirt, Victoria's purple glow flickering in and out, flashing desperately as they went.

Harriet was panting, leaning over what was left of the railing. She raised her hands, taking in a breath, as if she was going to shoot another spell towards them, but then relaxed again, realizing there was no use. They were already tumbling across the fields, so far away now that Amelia could make out nothing but Victoria's flashing aura.

"No," Harriet breathed. "*No!*" She kicked the railing in rage and it toppled over with her force, falling down into the garden. She gripped her head in her hands.

Amelia had been stunned into silence, watching as the wolf and Victoria faded out of view. "How could she have found us?"

Harriet spun towards Sam. "She must have followed *you!*"

"We teleported!" Sam cried in protest. "How could she?"

Harriet opened her mouth, but no words came and she grunted in frustration.

"Pointing fingers won't do us any good," said Amelia, still dumbstruck. "We have to...we have to make a plan. We can't just leave him. We can't just let Victoria get away with this."

But as she said these words, even she was not sure of what they meant. At that moment, she was also very aware that Peter may have just saved her life.

Suddenly, Dominic, who had simply been sitting helpless on the ground, had stood up, his face flushed red, and cried, "*I'm telling my mum!*"

"*Dominic!*" Harriet growled, but he was already off, running across the rubble to the inside of the house. Shortly after he did, another head slowly rose up from the crumbling staircase.

Sofia stood there, her jaw slightly ajar, blinking at them cluelessly. And for the first time in her life, as the witch looked upon the aftermath and wreckage, Amelia heard her swear.

All Was Lost

The witches' first instinct was to flee once again, and it left all of them uneasy to remain in the same place where Victoria had found them. But they could not in good conscience leave the Chesterfields to face Victoria's wrath. Before dawn broke, they took it upon themselves to lace the house with the proper charms—despite the protests of Harriet's mother.

"I honestly don't see the point, dears," the witch complained. "Perhaps if one of you would explain who exactly that witch on the roof really *was* we could simply come to an agreement with her. We're all civilized people, aren't we?"

"No, mother," Harriet replied irritatedly as she collected her spare talismans and crystals. "Not the word I would use."

The witch looked upon the remnants of her desecrated garden and muttered to herself as if no one else could hear, "I knew I never should have let that mangy wolf in the house. Now look at what that horrid creature has done."

Amelia was not quite sure how to describe the expression that made its way onto Harriet's face, the shock and disgust that contorted her features.

"What did you say?" she asked, her voice suddenly cold.

"It's my own fault, really," her mother went on, shaking her head sadly. "I should never have trusted one of them to sit at our table. You invite them in once, and suddenly they think they belong."

Harriet froze where she stood, the talismans clinking in her hands. Amelia could see her knuckles whiten around the string of charms, as though it was only their sharp edges keeping her from exploding.

"*One of them?*" she repeated. Her voice was quiet, but so precise that Amelia almost flinched. "You mean Peter. You mean the boy who nearly got himself killed last night when he saved Amelia. When he saved our family."

Her mother waved a dismissive hand, as though brushing away an unpleasant smell. "Oh, I'm sure he meant well. But intentions don't change blood, Harriet. Wolves are dangerous. That's their nature."

The air seemed to shift. The protective wards strung across the beams hummed faintly, and Amelia couldn't tell if it was the magic or Harriet's fury that made her hair prickle at the roots.

"Dangerous?" Harriet's laugh was short, incredulous. "He's *the only reason* any of us are still alive. He's worth more than your entire perfect little garden."

Her mother's face tightened. "Mind your tongue, girl."

But Harriet had already stepped closer, her eyes burning. "No. You don't get to sneer at him after everything he's done. You don't get to pretend your fear makes you right. Peter is our friend, and if you can't see past your own prejudice, then you don't deserve the protection we're giving you."

The room fell silent, broken only by the quiet hum of the charms Sofia had just tied against the doorframe. Amelia caught herself holding her breath, heart quickening at the look on Harriet's face—like she'd set something loose that couldn't be taken back.

"Just like you, Harry, to make it all about *you.*"

Millie had come into the room, leaning lazily at the threshold. "We don't need your lousy coven to protect us, you know." She glanced at Amelia and the others. "No offense, of course," she said, though it clearly was.

Harriet didn't even flinch this time. She turned to face her cousin fully, her expression steady, her shoulders squared. "You really don't get it, do you, Mills?"

Millie arched a brow, smirking. "Get what? That you've been playing witchling with your little friends while the rest of us deal with reality?"

Harriet's eyes never left Millie's. "The reality is that things have changed. *I've* changed."

Millie snorted. "Sure. You've got a few new tricks. Doesn't make you special."

The talisman string Harriet had been clutching glowed faintly in her hand, responding to the surge in her chest. A pulse of heat and light made the air shimmer. Amelia saw Millie's smirk falter for the first time.

"You think I'm weak because that's easier for you," Harriet said, her voice quiet but ringing with steel. "Because if I'm weak, then you're still the strong one. And if I'm not weak, then I'm crazed and unruly, and you're the poised and *obedient* one. But here's the truth: I don't need your approval. I don't need your permission. And I'm not afraid of you. I never have been."

The wards overhead gave a soft crackle, like they too were listening. Millie pushed off the doorframe, trying to look unfazed, but her gaze darted—just once—to the light sparking in Harriet's palm.

"You're bluffing," she muttered, though her voice had lost its edge.

Harriet took one step closer, her power steady now, controlled. "Try me."

For a long, taut moment, they just stared at each other—the old pattern of their lives teetering, threatening to snap. And then, for the very first time, Millie looked away.

Amelia released a breath. The room felt different now, charged and new, as if Harriet had redrawn its boundaries with nothing more than her voice.

Harriet stepped back, and the hum of magic around them eased. "We're leaving," she announced. "Good luck floating out of this."

Harriet did not say another word for the whole walk back. In fact, none of them did. Amelia hadn't realized how they had all grown accustomed to Peter's presence. It felt strange without him, and even stranger to not know what had become of him.

There was a question buzzing through each of their minds. No one asked it out loud, for none of them had the answer. What were they to do? What *could* they do? They may not have been any more exposed than before, but they were certainly all more aware of it now. Victoria could appear around any given corner and the country was crawling with hunters out to kill them all. Even Peter might be a danger to them now in his current form. Not to mention that Elena had most certainly noticed their absence by now, and who knew what she planned to do about it? And what of Amelia's mother? If she knew they'd run away, she would be worried sick!

Nothing like impending doom, thought Amelia miserably.

The four girls each settled onto the bus stop bench, which protested weakly beneath their weight. It smelled like onions and mildew at the stop—but perhaps blaming the stop wasn't entirely fair, considering most of them hadn't been able to shower since they left home. (Somehow Sam always smelled like cinnamon and honey.)

Amelia didn't want to think about Sam. Or rather she couldn't. It was like every time she tried to replay those moments on the roof in her mind, she came up to some large brick wall that blocked her view. Did she even hear what she thought she'd heard? What did it mean? Did Sam know how much she'd heard? Each of these questions echoed through the wall but dissipated before she could come to any real conclusions. They hadn't made eye contact since they'd left the Chesterfield home. Maybe that was for the best. Maybe not. She wasn't sure of anything at this point.

A bus rumbled past without stopping, a roar that made Amelia flinch. None of them moved to wave it down.

Finally, Sam broke the silence. "We have to find Peter," she said, her voice unsteady. "He'll be human by now, right? He has to be."

"Unless the hunters got to him first," Harriet muttered darkly.

Sofia set her hand on Harriet's knee, and at first Amelia expected her to chastise the girl for her rashness. But she just kept her hand there and squeezed. There was something to that action, something deeper than Amelia could quite understand.

"What exactly happened to him?" Sam asked. "Did the full moon make him lose himself? Do you think he understood what was happening?"

Sofia thought for a moment. "All werewolves turn more wolf than human beneath the full moon, but I've read that it's more difficult for the younger ones."

"He knew what he was doing," Amelia stated. "He was protecting us. I saw it."

Sam's eyes finally flicked toward her, but only for a second. That single glance was enough to unravel Amelia all over again.

"Then we have to look for him," Sam said again.

"Where would we even look?" snapped Harriet. "We don't know anything! He could be halfway to the city already."

"She's right," Amelia agreed. "It's too dangerous."

"As if that's ever stopped us before," muttered Sam, but she leaned back and crossed her arms, looking away resigned.

Her words hung heavy in the cold air. Amelia's throat tightened, her hands curling uselessly in her lap. She wanted to say something—anything—to close the distance between them.

The sun finally crested the horizon, spilling pale gold light across the street. It should have felt like relief. Instead, it only made the shadows under their eyes more visible.

For the first time, Amelia wondered if this was it. If this was where their story ended—not in magic or triumph, but in silence, fear, and the unbearable weight of everything left unsaid.

The Endless Wood

"Enough," said Sofia, silencing yet another argument. "Peter or no Peter, bus or no bus, I still need supplies. I'm out of arrowroot."

"We are not going into the woods," Amelia insisted. Although it was now daytime, the thought of being surrounded by so many trees, enclosed in such a small yet endless space with Victoria somewhere near left her terribly uneasy. "If you need arrowroot, grow some here yourself."

"There's no soil," said Sofia. "I may be a witch, but I don't perform miracles. If I'm going to be growing very specific herbs in places they aren't native to, I'll at least need fertile soil. Trust me, I'd rather not take the risk, but I need herbs for our protective charms and spells."

"We've gotten this far without them," Harriet pointed out.

Sofia shot her a look. "I've been casting them since we left home, Harry."

The other witch went silent.

"Right." Sofia straightened her shirt. "I understand if you don't all want to come with me, but I would appreciate it if at least one of you would come take watch."

They seemed to share a collective sigh, and then, to everyone's surprise, they all spoke in unison:

"I will."

Sofia beamed. "Lovely."

So the coven trudged their way into the woods. Amelia couldn't help but notice that Sam now walked the closest to her that she had since they were at the Chesterfields', and wondered if she was more anxious than she let on.

The woods seemed endless. Even though she knew where they had come from, when she turned back, it all looked the same in every direction, like a tunnel of mirrors. At last Sofia settled on one spot, a small mound of damp soil that she marveled at as if it were gold. "This should do," she said as her hands began to glow around the spot. "It will just be a moment. I have to get all the components right."

It ended up taking longer than a moment, and Harriet was the first to announce she was done waiting. "We're still quite close to the house. I'm going to look around and see if Peter left a trail."

"Stay close," Sofia warned absentmindedly as she worked.

Harriet wandered off, and soon Sam turned towards the other direction. "I'll go this way. Cover more ground. Y'know."

Amelia hesitated. "I'll go with you."

Sam flinched, but said nothing in protest, nodding her head before walking off. Amelia trailed behind her, for some reason still nervous to get close. Was she angry with her? Was that why she felt such a distance? Sam's eyes were fixed straight ahead, her jaw tight, more tense than Amelia had ever seen her. Branches snapped beneath their feet, punctuating the silence.

Amelia glanced back, making sure they were out of earshot, and finally spoke. "Sam..."

Sam cut her off before she could even begin. "You don't have to say anything. I know."

How could Sam know what she was going to say, if Amelia herself was hardly sure? The thing was, Amelia wasn't even certain of what she'd heard on the rooftop. But she knew they couldn't let it just hang over both their heads until it all came crumbling down.

"Know what?" asked Amelia, trying to keep up so that she could at least get a look at her face, growing more and more frustrated.

"That you heard me." Sam quieted. "And I shouldn't have said it anyway. It was stupid. It was a mistake. Sorry."

"No, it—Sam."

Sam had quickened her pace and Amelia, without thinking, grabbed her wrist to hold her back.

"It didn't sound like a mistake."

That made Sam freeze and her eyes finally met the other girl's. Then she seemed to regain her bearings. "You don't have to pretend. You don't have to do all this to make me feel better." Her words were clipped, but they felt hollow and her cheeks were flushed with shame or shyness.

"I'm not pretending. I just...I don't know what I'm supposed to say. You've always been—Sam, you've always been—" She cut herself off, frustrated. It was as if what she meant to say was right at the tip of her tongue, but she was so sorely lacking in vocabulary. It was an exam she hadn't studied for, a book she hadn't had the time yet to read.

Meanwhile, Sam seemed to have only hardened more, as if what Amelia said had only confirmed everything she thought. She pulled her wrist away. "It's doomed," she breathed, more to herself than anyone else.

"Nothing is *doomed.*"

"I can see it in your eyes!" Sam exclaimed. "You feel sorry for me! You always have. You feel sorry for me now because of..." she gulped. "Because of what I said on the roof. You felt sorry for me when my dad died. You felt sorry for me when I didn't have any magic and you did. You felt sorry for me because I didn't have a mom and you did. You felt sorry for me since the day we met, because I wasn't smart like you were—because I've always been the friend you go to when you want to laugh, but not good enough to keep around for long." Her eyes had begun to cloud with tears, her nose already a bright shade of pink. She laughed humorlessly, a strained and wet sound. "That's the only reason I'm even here. You fought so hard for me to be able to come to Spain to train to be a witch. Because you felt bad for me."

"That's not—" Amelia began.

"Well, I'm not a witch!" Sam cried, birds fluttering from the branches above, startled by the noise.

"That doesn't mean anything!" Amelia insisted. "It makes no difference to me."

Sam shook her head, tears dripping down her cheeks. "Of course it doesn't. It doesn't make a difference to anyone. I might as well not be here."

Amelia's chest ached. She hated hearing her talk about herself in such a way. She hated it more than anything. "You're wrong."

Sam blinked, startled by the harshness of her voice.

"You're wrong," Amelia repeated, stepping closer. "You think I kept you around because I felt *sorry* for you? No. I kept you around because you make me *happy.* Because when everything is falling apart, you're the one person I want next to me. I look at you and I feel like I'm home. I look at you and sometimes the world just...shuts off. Like nothing else matters." Her hands had curled into fists without realizing. "Because it doesn't."

The truth was, sometimes Amelia was startled by just how much she thought about Sam, by just how much she would *do* for her. It had never been the guilt that had made Amelia fight to bring Sam to Spain nor the fear that Sam wouldn't do well on her own. Who was she kidding? The girl would have had a new best friend within a week. She would have gone right back to her books and TV shows that she loved and then gone back to school and lit up every room she was in. Sam would always be fine. There were few environments in which she wouldn't thrive. Amelia feared for *herself.* It was an ugly, selfish, desperate need. For how could she live without Sam by her side? How could she have entered that whole new world with a piece of her soul missing?

Sam's breath caught. She stared at Amelia, her jaw open, as if the ground had shifted beneath her feet.

The words tumbled out, fast and clumsy. "I don't feel sorry for you, Sam. I—" She faltered, cheeks burning. She still had not found the word. It still would not come.

And then a voice echoed through the gaps in the trees and she stopped. She couldn't tell from which direction the sound had come, but it seemed to multiply, one person's speech turning into three, a cacophony of chattering teenagers. But wait—she knew those voices!

The trio from the London bus were stumbling over branches and bushes, each of them speaking at once. A slight-framed goth girl, a round-faced vampire, and a tall boy with glasses.

"Well it's not *my* fault," hissed Millicent.

"I didn't say it was," replied the vampire calmly.

"If she won't, I will," quipped the boy.

Amelia glanced at Sam, their conversation far from forgotten, but with one look they agreed this was not something they could leave alone. Amelia looked back at the trio across the way as Millicent caught sight of them.

"Hey!" the girl shouted in all her apparent subtlety. "Witches!"

"*Shhh!*" hissed Amelia as they neared. "What are you doing here?"

Millicent crossed her arms defiantly. "I could ask you the same thing."

Amelia stared at her.

The vampire piped up from behind her. "We're lost." Millicent spun around and tried to slap a hand over her mouth, but it was too late.

When she turned, Amelia spotted something at the edge of her shirt, a dark stain that had bloomed across the entire half of her back. She gasped involuntarily.

Sam pointed it out before Amelia could. "You're covered in *blood.*"

Millicent rolled her eyes. "Yeah, well, it's not mine. We ran into some beast last night while trying to run from this pack of witch hunters—the savage bastards."

"You saw witch hunters?" asked Amelia.

The vampire spoke up again. "Only a couple of them. A bunch of amateurs, really. But they found us with this strange device they've stolen from the GMUC." She rolled her eyes as if the act was so juvenile. "Anyway, the beast got to them eventually. Ate their limbs like drumsticks. But one made it out alive and we asked him about the device. It got smushed in the fight, but get this—they broke in through—"

"*Shuuuush!*" hissed Millicent once more. "We can't go around telling just anyone how to break into the bloody GMUC!"

"What are they going to do, hm?" asked the vampire. "They're kids."

"We're fourteen," argued Sam.

"Yes, exactly," the vampire agreed. Sam frowned.

"Wait," Amelia stopped them, eyeing the large circle of blood. "What kind of beast?"

"Some sort of werewolf, I suppose, I—" The girl suddenly paused mid sentence, her eyes slowly drifting towards Amelia, whose face had been drained of all color. "Hey, weren't you lot hanging with a wolf on the train?"

Another voice came from the woods, this one much more familiar to Amelia.

"Amelia, Sam, get over here! I think I found pawprints in the—" Harriet suddenly stopped upon catching sight of the trio. "What the bloody hell are they doing here?"

"Watch your tongue," barked Millicent and a dim glow began to pulsate from her fists. Amelia had learned to recognize a witch's aura, and this girl's, although dim, was certainly that.

"I have an idea," said Amelia, placing herself between them. "Why don't we all be calm for a moment and not blow each other up?" Oh, how she wished she had the diplomatic ability of Sofia. (Speaking of whom, where *was* Sofia?)

Harriet looked her up and down. "It's cute how you put yourself in my line of fire. As if I wouldn't blast you, too."

Amelia chose to ignore her. "Harry, they found Peter."

That drew her attention, something coming alight in the witch's eyes. "What? Where? What happened?"

Sofia, as if sensing her presence was needed, appeared from behind a tree. She was in her element, as if she was simply part of the woods. Her hair blended with the weaving bark of tree trunks, her tan arms with the branches. She took in the scene before her, not quite concerned, but rather interested and intrigued. "What is this?"

The vampire began to speak once more, and this time, Millicent did not stop her. Her name turned out to be Elizabeth (but her friends called her Ellie, and they all could, too—if they'd like), and the story as she told it went like this: They had been trekking along the side of the road, on their way up North to stay with Andrew's family (that was the boy with the glasses) when they'd heard noise from within the woods and had gone to investigate. They saw a magical glow and so they thought what they would find were other witches, but instead they were met with that tiny band of witch hunters—who were no match for what would come next.

"The beast and this crazed witch came *barreling in*," Millicent cut in. "The witch disappeared before we could get a good look at her, but there was something about her that just..." She shuddered. "She wasn't right. I've got a second sense for dark magic, I tell you."

"Go on," Harriet urged Ellie, the vampire.

So she did. She explained how after the werewolf had attacked the hunters, he turned towards Ellie and her friends, forcing them to run. But it seemed to be bleeding, and eventually tired out, never catching up.

"And that's how we ended up here. Lost." Ellie sighed.

"We're not lost," argued Millicent. "I'm telling you, the road is right back over there."

"We are lost," the boy, Andrew, agreed with a grave nod.

"We can lead you back to the road," Sofia offered right away, and they lit up in response, but she spoke again. "On one condition."

Andrew blinked. "So, you're holding us hostage?"

Sofia ignored the question. "That witch you saw—she's after us. The wolf is our friend. We want you to help us find them both."

Just as the trio was about to respond, most likely in protest, Sam gasped with some sort of divine epiphany. They all turned to her, startled.

"The blood is Peter's!" she squeaked, still staring at Millicent's clothes.

"Yeah, we established that, Red," Millicent began.

"No, it's—No, I know what to do." She looked up, finger to her lips. "I know what to do!"

Blood Magic

As boring as Sam had found Elena's Caster training to be thus far, it turned out that not all of it was limited to pretty charms and unintelligible Latin phrases. In fact, one of the first things she had read up on was the use of blood magic. Elena had forced her to memorize the acronym by heart: DRAT. (Divination, Rituals, Amplification, and Tracking.) None of the first three had come up yet, but tracking was exactly what they needed now.

So Sam had Millicent sit down on the grass as she bent over her, inspecting the bloodstain across the front of her shirt. It was too dry to wring out, but when they poured water over the fabric and let it drip into a glass jar, Sofia offered up her arrowroot to cast a purification spell on the murky pink liquid until it became thick, crimson blood. And then she got to work, carving a rune around the jar in the moist dirt as the smell of iron permeated the air. Next, she took a needle and carefully pricked her own finger before letting a drop of blood fall into the jar with Peter's.

"Magic needs a bridge, you see," said Sam, who was realizing that for the first time *she* was the sole expert on this type of magic. Finally, she was able to do something on her own, and the others just watched in amazement as the jar began to shudder and shake with magic.

She gripped the jar to hold it still and closed her eyes. "*Sanguis sequens.*" At first nothing happened. She had never been the best at verbal incantations, but it was the words that would trigger the spell into action. Without them, it could not be cast and the magic wouldn't go anywhere. "*Sanguis sequens,*" she spoke again. She felt a slight pull, but it only lasted a moment and she couldn't tell where it meant to lead.

"*Sanguis sequens,*" she said once more, her voice holding a desperate quality.

Just as she was about to speak the two words once more, Sofia suddenly leaned down and placed a hand around Sam's. The two girls spoke at the same time:

"*Sanguis sequens.*"

The jar instantly burst into light and they both went stumbling back with the force of its magic. The path was visible at once. The spell had formed what looked to be a glowing trail of light that lined the forest floor, glittering and pulsing with the spell's power.

Sam burst into triumphant laughter, holding her stomach as she leaned back. "We did it!" She looked up at Sofia. "How did you do that?"

Sofia grinned shyly and shrugged. "I've always had powerful incantations. That is, verbal magic. My father is half elf, and elves specialize in incantations. I suppose I inherited that and not the ears." She tapped her own rounded ears with her finger.

Harriet grabbed Sofia by the ears and pulled her down to give her a fat kiss on the head. "Sofi, you're brilliant."

Sofia blushed with embarrassment. Harriet was already off, trailing down the glowing path. The other trio shared a glance among themselves, perhaps considering their options, and then reluctantly followed after the witch.

That left Sofia, Amelia, and Sam, standing in the open clearing as the birds and leaves rustled around them.

For a beat, Sofia lingered. She opened her mouth as if to say something, then paused, her gaze flicking between the two of them. Slowly, her eyebrows arched. A dawning look of realization spread across her face.

"Well then," she muttered, almost too low to hear, and with a suspiciously brisk turn on her heel, she marched off down the path. She didn't so much as glance back.

And then there were two.

Sam was still kneeling on the ground before the jar. She was looking up at Amelia, her honey brown eyes round and wide.

Amelia was thinking of nothing but their conversation from before. That, and Sam's eyes. She was faced with a feeling she had never felt before that made her body tense and her heart slam against her ribs. Sam rose slowly off the ground and met her at her level.

The wind brushed through the girl's red hair and strewed it across her face, catching at her lips. Amelia raised her hand instinctually to pull it away, and then stopped herself. She began to pull her hand back, but Sam took it, and brought it to her face.

Amelia was met with the warmth of Sam's skin, the soft flesh of her cheeks, and then the edge of her mouth. She pulled the loose tendrils of red hair away from her lips and gulped, hoping that the other girl didn't see how her hands shook so much.

Sam placed her hand over Amelia's and held it there on her cheek, her eyes lazily falling closed. She looked happy there, like she could stay there for hours, perfectly content. But Amelia's head still swam. The morning light from above was peeking through the leaves, scattering across her freckles like gold. Sam didn't look human at that moment. She looked like a painting or the statue of an ancient deity. Amelia was not worthy to be gazing upon her at eye level; that face was one meant to be observed while on your knees.

Before fully understanding what she was doing, she moved forward.

Her breath hitched, caught halfway in her throat, but Sam didn't pull back. She tilted ever so slightly forward, her forehead brushing against Amelia's like it was the most natural thing in the world.

For a moment, Amelia thought she might faint from how hard her heart was beating. Her mind screamed that she didn't know how to do this, didn't even know if she *should*. But Sam's hand was still warm against hers.

Their noses bumped and Amelia almost laughed. But then Sam's lips found hers, light as a whisper. It was a trembling press of one breath against another, but the entire forest had gone silent to listen.

The kiss ended almost before it began. Amelia pulled back just a fraction, wide-eyed, as if she'd stepped off the edge of a cliff and somehow had landed on her feet. Sam lingered close, still holding her hand to her cheek, still glowing faintly in the dappled morning light.

Amelia had the distinct feeling that this was what real magic felt like. That no spell could ever come close.

The blood trail drew them deeper into the woods, but not as far as Amelia expected. Soon enough, the trail began to dissipate and fade into the crumbled leaves and grass of the forest floor.

"Does that mean he's close?" asked Harriet.

"I think so," replied Sam. And so they began their search, both the coven and the trio fanning out to cover more ground.

"Here!" Softia called out and they all crowded around.

It wasn't a wolf they found lying unconscious in the grass, but a boy. Peter had no fangs or claws. His chest was covered with brown, crusted blood, his hair an unruly mat that fell over his eyes. The grass and branches around him seemed to cradle him, as if the forest itself was there to protect him.

Also, he was naked.

Amelia stepped back, covering her eyes. "Oh. Um."

The other girls looked equally clueless, except for Harriet, who rolled her eyes with annoyance at them all.

"Oh, please," she groaned before untying the plaid shirt at her waist and throwing it over the boy. She bent down to inspect the wound across his chest. "Sofi, come look at this. It's definitely magic-inflicted." She took hold of his shoulders and tried to jostle him awake. "Peter."

"Hold on, I have a potion for this," Sam said suddenly, her eyes wide as if she had only just registered that she could in fact be useful. She kneeled down beside Harriet and Peter and from her pocket she plucked a strange little jar made of green glass that curled and bent in odd ways, like a colony of algae. She rubbed her hands together and blew a breath of air into the bottle.

Amelia watched her with fascination. How had she missed this? It was as if she had blinked and Sam had become more of a witch than she, manipulating the magic potion in her hands like it was second nature. Within moments, Sam was pouring the sizzling green liquid over the jagged gashes in Peter's chest, which rose and fell with shallow breath.

Sam tucked the potion away and waited. The forest went silent in anticipation.

Finally, the potion began to do its work, the green glow spreading across his skin, eating away at the scabs forming on his skin. At first, its light glimmered across the wound, but slowly as it faded, the clear, undamaged skin was revealed. Amelia sighed in relief.

Peter's breaths grew stronger and quickly turned to groans. His eyes fluttered open and he looked around with confusion. "What's...going? Huh?"

"Is he always this articulate?" asked Millicent.

"He's incapacitated," Ellie chastised her.

Peter groped at his own chest, still glittering with green light. "Am I dying?"

"No." Sam snorted. "Hold still, weirdo."

"What happened?" he asked, relaxing as the magic did its work.

"You turned into a wolf," she told him.

He blinked blankly at her for a moment, and then, without warning, he pumped a fist in the air. "*Finally!*"

"You also nearly killed several people," Amelia pointed out.

"Oh." He lowered his fist. "Sorry."

"Water under the bridge," Millicent muttered, though she didn't seem to completely mean it.

Unfortunately, their moment of reprieve wasn't meant to last. They still had a mission.

"Millicent," said Amelia. Her voice held the extent of her determination, and the group went silent. Millicent looked at her, arching her needle-thin brows. "Tell us again about the witch hunters. Their magic-detecting device. How did you say they got a hold of it?"

At first, the girl raised a brow at her, unsure, but then she began to speak.

195

The Ironworker Union

Witches had existed in legend for thousands of years, but magic itself was an element as old as water and air. Witches were simply conduits, women born with the talent to harness magic. And there was a reason they had lived on despite centuries of men, witch hunters, and colonists trying to eliminate them. The concept of an autonomous magical government had been an integral part of witch culture throughout history, but the Government of Magic or Unusual Creatures itself was a relatively new institution, originating in the late nineteenth century disguised as *the Ironworker Union 88.*

All this, Amelia knew from her textbooks for Elena's classes. What she had not yet realized was that it was because the GMUC was such a new organization that it was so vulnerable. And witches may have been old, but men's hatred was older.

This was why the GMUC had inevitably earned its flaws. There was always a crack in the system, if one just knew where to look. This chip in the grand institution's armor had a name. Archibald.

Archibald was a middle aged, overly-polite, and slightly effeminate English telepath who had only two jobs. His first duty was to the GMUC, monitoring all those who entered the magic-free sector of the building through the very advanced security system (a washroom which turned into an elevator once one was granted entry by Archibald himself). This involved a thorough background check of each witch, elf or goblin who requested entry before lowering the contraption down into the GMUC headquarters, and then taking meticulous record of every individual who did so, that way preventing even the most miniscule possibility of foul play.

Archibald's second duty, however, was to a group who referred to themselves as the Order of the Cleansing Flame.

But to the magical population of London, they were known simply as the witch hunters.

The entire story of just how Archibald had come to band together with the group of bloodthirsty witch hunters was long and complicated (and Millicent had never got around to asking the witch hunter whom she'd tortured much about it) but what mattered was that he was there every day from nine in the morning to five in the afternoon, resting behind a gap in a bathroom mirror and controlling a magical portal that only opened when the proper spell was cast by someone inside the bathroom. Obviously, he could not see through the other side of the mirror unless said spell was cast. That would be creepy.

Unfortunately, what he did was much more malicious than spying on people in bathrooms. The dark secret was that the man had been aiding his witch hunter friends for years. One of his more notable feats in this long and carefully-handled alliance was his acquisition of dozens of outdated magic detectors which had been scheduled for disposal.

This was the story of how the Order of the Cleansing Flame, the amateur hunter's group in London, had come into the possession of a magic detector, which they had later used to track down Millicent and her crew—before its prompt destruction.

It was also the story of how the Hummingbird Coven realized what could be their salvation.

"He told me there was a code," said Millicent. "That they recite some poem and this Archibald bloke will let you through."

"If we can do this," began Amelia, "then we can get to the time machine prototype that Diana told us about. And then if we can get it to work like Victoria did, we can finally put an end to this. We'll just go back to the past and change things. Change the past to change the future."

"A bit convoluted, don't you think?" said Harriet.

"I second that," Millicent agreed.

Amelia ignored them. "There's one problem."

"Only one?" asked Harriet.

"None of us look like witch hunters." Amelia gestured to them all, prompting everyone to take in their own appearances. It was true; even Ellie, technically the oldest out of the eight of them, looked to be only a preteen. None of them could pass for adults and hardly matched the stereotype of a bloodthirsty bigoted witch hunter. "Not to mention, this man, Archibald, will know if we're lying. You said he's a telepath."

"We know the code," argued Harriet. "I say we take our chances."

Amelia felt queasy at the idea of such a risk, but what choice did they have? "Well, we can't all go in. It would be too suspicious. And one of us will have to tell him the code without giving anything away."

"I'll do it," volunteered Harriet.

"You don't exactly have a poker face," Amelia stated bluntly. Harriet twisted her lips, clearly offended, which only proved her point.

"Then I'll do it," said Sofia, standing a little taller than before. They all looked at her and she seemed to bristle. "I know a thing or two about telepaths. I've read up on the art of reading minds. I can do my best to try and fool him."

"Okay, girlie." Millicent laughed condescendingly. "I don't think that's how it works."

"Hey," Harriet snapped coldly. "If Sofi says she can do it, then she can do it." She turned back to Sofia, and as they shared a look, the witch beamed with pride.

"Well, then," said Amelia, sucking in a steadying breath. "I guess it's time for a heist."

Her gaze fell on Sam out of habit. Something had changed about her. Whether it was more Amelia's perception than anything else, she didn't know, but one thing was true—light seemed to radiate off of her like the sun, a new and determined glint in her eye.

Amelia wasn't sure what they were getting themselves into, but she knew they would be ready for whatever came next.

For some reason, Amelia had expected the GMUC building in London to be a shopping mall, just like in Spain. But what they found was a building which looked to be a very modern museum at first. It was a large and bulky structure with banners and advertisements strewn across the facade with an endless garden maze that stretched before them, leading to the wide entrance of wooden and marble doors. Across the top of them was etched in big letters *THE MAGICAL LONDON WAX MUSEUM.*

"Isn't that kind of on-the-nose?" asked Amelia.

"Because I'm sure if a couple months ago you saw a wax museum called magical, you'd immediately assume it was the secret hideout of a witch's society," Harriet droned, her voice dripping with sarcasm.

"Fair point," Amelia replied. "Okay. The eight of us will draw too much attention if we all go in at once. Will you three keep watch?" She looked at Millicent, Ellie, and Andrew.

"Gladly," said Andrew, and the other two nodded enthusiastically. The fact that they were so excited to *not* be going inside did not improve Amelia's confidence.

The longer they stood in that spot, the larger the building seemed to grow, but she pushed her nerves down and moved forward. When they stepped inside the wax museum, Amelia was greeted not by wonders or enchantments, but by an odd stillness mixed with the smell of disinfectant and dust. Every figure in the lobby had that glassy-eyed, frozen expression that seemed a little too lifelike the longer you stared.

A man in a top hat stood mid-bow with one arm outstretched. A pair of Victorian ladies clutched lace fans to their chests, looking forever scandalized. A wax replica of Queen Elizabeth blinked at them from across the room (or seemed to, until Amelia realized it was just her own nerves.)

"This isn't creepy at all," muttered Peter.

"Harry's sarcasm is rubbing off on you," Amelia whispered to him.

They moved along the polished tile floors, past rows of wax figures frozen in tea parties, coronations, duels. The longer Amelia stared, the more she swore she saw their chests rising, their eyes twitching, as if waiting for the exact wrong moment to move.

It was Sam who eventually broke the silence: "Do we... uh, know where we're going?"

Amelia spotted it then, the glorious glowing sign in the corner down the hall in the shape of a shining, white toilet. "There."

The girls and Peter scampered quietly down the dusty carpet and made their way into the bathroom one by one, and soon found themselves very cramped, as the room was (in theory) made for only one occupant. As Amelia ducked inside, she thought she glimpsed a tour guide standing by one of the figures giving them all an awfully funny look.

Amelia shut the door firmly behind them, enclosing them in utter darkness for a moment before Sofia successfully found the light switch. Their gazes all fell on the bathroom mirror at the front of the room, which reflected back nothing but their own nervous expressions.

"You know the spell?" Amelia asked Sofia, remembering how Elena had let them in last time.

"It won't be necessary," Sofia said, shaking her head. "Not everyone coming into the GMUC is a witch, after all."

She reached forward and knocked gently on the glass with her fist.

The glass shimmered and warped for a moment and then slowly the image of the five of them faded away and was replaced by a man sitting behind the glass. He was a thin man with almost claw-like fingers which he used to swat a strand of gray hair from his forehead back into its slicked-back position. He wore a very formal-looking tie with puppies printed across it. His eyes were bright white, marking him as a telepath. He sniffed, hardly looking up from his desk.

"Name and purpose for your visit," he requested flatly in a nasally British drawl, clearly having been reciting the same script for hours.

"Ophelia Carmen Fernández," Sofia stated, her chest puffed up and her chin high, as confident and calm as if she'd done this a million times over already.

The man's telepath-white eyes snapped up like she'd just said something very shocking. "Is that so? Purpose?"

Sofia had told them it was imperative that they all keep their minds very blank, and that any sudden movement or sign of panic in their mind would draw attention. So she thought of the most neutral things she could muster. Lukewarm water. White bread. Switzerland. The color beige. The smell of honey. Freckles. Sa—No, not Sam.

"We're with the cleaning crew." Sofia's voice was still cool and calm, her eyes never leaving the telepath's.

At first, the telepath didn't answer. He seemed to be taking her in, still determining his judgement. But then finally, he vanished and the reflection returned. Amelia heard Sofia release a shuddering breath.

"Did we do it?" Sam whispered softly.

Sofia held up a finger for her to wait, and then as if in response the room began to move. The floor shifted beneath their feet. The bathroom had turned into an elevator and they were moving downwards. Amelia bit her lip, containing her triumph. When she caught Sofia's gaze, she nodded with approval.

"How did you do it?" asked Peter curiously as they continued moving down.

"With a clear enough mind, anything's possible," said Sofia. "That and a dozen mental shields in place beforehand." She plucked a glowing leaf out from behind her ear.

"Are you sure he understood?" asked Sam

Sofia nodded. "Ophelia Carmen Fernández. OCF. The same as the Order of the Cleansing Flame, which is the organization that witch hunter in the woods was from. It's also why I said we were here to clean—or cleanse, as the case may be."

Amelia cringed. "Ew."

"It was our way in," Sofia replied, though from the look on her face it seemed that she agreed.

The room's descent came to a stop and the walls began to shift, each brick sliding out of place and coming apart with a deep rumble. The wall slid open like doors, revealing a long, open hallway before them.

"It looks just like the GMUC back home," Amelia said softly.

The hallway was a sleek tunnel of white stone with marble pillars leading all the way down to an end which she could not make out. The ceilings curved artfully above them in an arching shape. But the glittering hallway was not what sent an uncanny discomfort running through her bones as they entered, but something else. She knew it would come this time, but still she found herself unprepared as the feeling of emptiness came over her. Nausea rose up in her stomach and a chill ran down her spine. That was the feeling of the iron around them, suppressing the magic within her. The air felt thicker, more difficult to suck in each breath.

"I don't think I'll ever get used to that," said Amelia.

"You don't," said Sofia. She looked a bit queasy herself—as did Harriet. Sam and Peter were the only ones unaffected.

"So, where do all of these doors lead?" asked Peter as they all made their way out of the bathroom. Once they were out, the wall slid firmly back into place and then closed up as if it had never been there at all.

Amelia looked down the endless hall, hundreds doors lining the way, each identical and spaced evenly apart. "Wherever we want them to," she answered and then turned to Sofia, who must have known everything about the place. "Right?"

"That's right," Sofia affirmed. "It may not be easy to get inside the GMUC, but it isn't difficult to navigate."

Since she was the one standing the closest, Sofia placed her hand on the first door handle and slowly turned it open. She began to move forward and then stopped once she saw was on the other side.

"Ah," she sighed. "It won't work if *I* do it."

"How come?" wondered Sam.

Sofia closed the door, the sound echoing softly through the hall. "Because I don't really want to be here."

"Fair enough," said Amelia, stepping forward. It wasn't that she particularly *did,* but considering Harriet would most likely lead them to somewhere less than desirable, Sam to some-where dark where she could lay down (judging by the heavy circles beneath her eyes), and Peter didn't seem like he really knew what was going on, Amelia would most likely be their best bet. And after all, a resolve had already begun to swell within her. They were going to do this. They were going to put an end to this fight with Victoria once and for all.

She closed her eyes and when she turned the door handle, thought clearly about what she needed, envisioning what the machine may look like in her mind, thinking of Victoria. She let the magic of the building do the rest.

When she opened her eyes she wasn't sure what exactly she would find. It was a cavernous chamber that looked like the inside of a cathedral if a cathedral had been gutted and rebuilt into a workshop. The ceiling arched so high it disap-peared into shadow, with iron catwalks crisscrossing above like spiderwebs. The air smelled faintly of oil and candlewax, a strange blend of mechanical grit and magic.

At the center of the room sat the machine. It wasn't sleek or elegant, but a hulking mess of brass cogs, grimy dials, and looping copper tubing, like a grandfather clock had exploded and been stitched back together by someone who didn't entirely know what they were doing. Runes shimmered faintly across its surface, flickering in and out of visibility as though even the enchantments themselves were unstable.

Workbenches surrounded it in a chaotic ring, cluttered with open books, quills that scribbled on their own, and tools both mundane and bizarre: wrenches with glowing teeth, saws that hummed like bees. Blueprints hung from the walls, curling at the edges, some drawn in precise ink, others smeared in chalk and annotated with scribbled notes.

But the strangest thing was the silence. Amelia had expected bustling magical engineers in overalls or cloaked mechanics murmuring spells over broken gears. Instead, the place was empty. Empty—but not abandoned. A mug of tea steamed gently on one of the benches, quills were still moving independently across parchment, and the great pendulum at the machine's core was swinging as if freshly wound.

The longer Amelia stood there, the stronger the sense of unease pressed against her ribs. The room wasn't still; it was holding its breath.

But she felt different, too. That pressing suffocation had loosened its grip on her. She turned to Sofia. "I can't feel the iron as much here."

"I think we're higher up," she said. "Probably to help the runes take effect. Look at the quills."

Amelia moved deeper into the room. There was so much to the machine that she wasn't sure where to look. All of the runes scrawled across it were new, a desecration done by the Casters on the machine Victoria had crafted—they'd carved into metal just to try and get it to work, for they could not speak Victoria's language, so they spoke in their own. Sam stood at her side, totally entranced, her eyes wide and glittering as she gazed upon the contraption. She raised a hand out as if to touch it but quickly pulled back.

"These Caster runes are..." Sam began, but was hardly capable of finishing her sentence. She laughed softly to herself. "I can barely understand half of them, they're so advanced."

Amelia had seen that look of wonder on the girl's face before, a kind of intrigue that could not be shaken.

"Do you think we could get it working?" Amelia asked her.

"I know I couldn't on my own," Sam replied, her confidence faltering.

Amelia reached for her hand and squeezed it tightly. "Well, you're not on your own." She looked out at the machine. With her magic, Sofia and Sam's knowledge, and Harriet's power, there had to be a way they could make it work. Diana believed in them. She could too.

Sam began to circle around the machine, trying not to trip over the loose wires and doohickeys as she took it all in. Amelia came closer and lifted her hand to the machine's surface, one metal plate devoid of the Caster's runes. When her skin came to contact with the machine, all that residual dull feeling within her, the pressing down of the iron's power, faded away. She gasped, looking down to the wires and lines drawn from the machine up and up through the walls. It wasn't just electricity that was running through it, but *magic* as well. She could feel it pulsing through her, and then when she pulled away, the iron pressed down once more.

But that surge of magic was enough. It really was like another language, for that feeling allowed her to see. Looking at the machine, she now understood it better, she could identify that port there at the edge—that was where you were meant to step in—and the lever at the bottom for activating it. That light along the sides would indicate stability. And the buzzing on the plate...It wasn't broken, she realized. It was responding to the rhythm of the pendulum. Like a heartbeat.

Her own magic tugged at her chest, answering back before she could stop it. Suddenly, the lines of copper tubing weren't random. They were veins. The gears were the ribs of a living thing holding the mechanism steady. Every jagged note of sound, every pulse of glow, was part of a rhythm she could feel deep in her bones.

Yes, it was most certainly Victoria who had built this machine. And it terrified her just how well she understood the witch's mind.

She lingered for a moment longer, getting a feel for the machine's parts, and then slowly something began to click. A tiny corner, a hidden edge called to her. Something was off there. If she could just tweak—

Her train of thought was interrupted by the sound of the door opening from behind them. She spun around.

"*There!*"

Two telepaths with bright white eyes barged into the room, pointing accusatory fingers at them as GMUC guards came up behind them, a long, glowing spear in each of their hands. They charged through the room and grabbed onto Harriet first.

"Hey!" she cried, baring her teeth and scratching wildly at them. Amelia saw the moment she instinctively reached for her magic, lifting a palm, only for it to falter into a flickering glow. One of the guards grabbed her arm and it went out completely before he clicked her arms in handcuffs. Still, she tried to wrench herself from the man's grip.

They came for Peter next, but he had no magic to reach for. The only power he had was one he could hardly control, and so although he tried to push away from the guard that came for him, the man lifted his spear and a magical blast shot out from the tip of it, stunning Peter instantly before he crumbled to the floor.

Her mind reeling, Amelia reached for the time machine again, thinking that if she could just get into contact with it again, she could use her magic and—

A blast hit her, grazing the tips of her fingers just before she could touch the metal of the machine. She recoiled, cradling her hand. When she looked down, she caught a glimpse of her old scar, the scar given to her by Matthew on that fateful night at the creek...and memories began to swell up in her, filling her with dread as she watched her friends be apprehended one by one.

One of the guards put his hands on Sam, wrenching her back by her shoulder as she clung desperately to the machine.

Amelia swung herself forward, fighting against the numb feeling across her muscles from the stun. She moved her whole body towards the machine and fell against it. Magic filled her instantly.

She tried to stop time, anything to give them another moment to fight, to get out of this. She watched as the scene before her started and stopped, her power flickering in and out. She could not raise her arms properly to focus any telekinetic force towards the guards. Perhaps if she had Harriet's fire she could use that to push them away, but as the energy in her body faded, so did her control.

She strained harder, trying to will the world around her to pause, but she was too late. One of the guards raised his spear once more and acting out of fear, she tried to move out of his line of fire. But she hadn't thought it through—she lost contact with the machine and time quickened again, giving the guard the opportunity to hit her with another blast.

And then the world went dark.

The Chance

Amelia woke in a strange, dark room. Must and mildew filled her nostrils. Distantly, there was a rhythmic tapping like water dripping. It took her a moment before she could open her eyes fully, all her systems terribly discombobulated.

"Sam?" The name left her lips before she could even think about it.

"Here," the reply came softly. She was close by. Amelia turned her head, taking in her surroundings.

If the GMUC had not looked like a basement before, it certainly did now. (That is, if they even *were* still in the GMUC) The wall was solid concrete, marked with old stains and scuffs. The rest of the room was blocked off by rows of metal bars, and then there was a door on the other side, gray and solid, with only one small glass window at the top. Amelia was sitting on the floor, her back propped up against the cold wall, and Sam was beside her, head hanging between her knees. Separated from them by another set of bars were Peter, Sofia, and Harriet. Sofia seemed barely conscious, rubbing her temples gently. Peter and Harriet were still knocked out. They had left Harriet handcuffed, her arms behind her back.

Amelia reached for the magic within her, but came up with nothing. She could feel that they were even farther beneath the earth here. There was no familiar buzz at her fingers, no hum in her chest. They were alone down there.

"Are you okay?" Amelia asked Sam, reaching for her hand.

Sam met her eyes and spoke weakly. "We failed."

"No." Amelia shook her head. "No, it isn't our fault. It'll be fine. We're in the GMUC. At least here, we're protected from *her.*"

"That's what you think." Harriet had woken up, her words slurred but still holding poison. "The GMUC is a bloody joke. They won't protect us." She began to laugh. "It must have been that dummy telepath in the mirror. He must have ratted us out."

"But he let us in," Sofia breathed in disbelief. "I thought I..." She trailed off.

"It's not your fault," said Amelia. "We'll make it out of this." She met Sam's gaze again. "I swear."

Sam looked down. Amelia couldn't tell if she believed her or not. Amelia wasn't even sure if she believed herself.

Harriet stood without warning, swayed for a moment, and then steadied. She approached the bars. "Maybe there's a way to break out."

"*Break out?*" Sofia echoed. "We're in enough trouble as is, Harry. My mother is going to murder me."

"It's a bit too late to worry about your mother, Sof."

Sofia had no retort.

Just then, that heavy metal door on the other side of the bars swung open.

And then the world seemed to turn on its head.

It was Victoria who stood at the threshold. She waltzed in as if it were perfectly normal, silence swallowing the room. She looked just as she had on the roof. None of the resolve within her had shaken. In fact, she seemed more smug now, her chin high, her gait almost lazy. But that look in her eye was something terrifying. Amelia was her prey, and already caught in a cage.

The door fell shut behind her. "Funny seeing you here."

None of them spoke. They were all doing the same thing, running through every possible action in their head, trying to imagine how this now played out. After all, they knew what she wanted. But they had no magic, no time machine, and no key to these wretched cages.

"What?" asked Victoria, holding her hands up. "No warm welcome? Hardly seems fair to your deal ol granny."

"Funny," Amelia replied flatly.

Victoria looked amused. "Well, it's not much of a joke, is it?"

Again, they all stayed silent. Peter was finally beginning to stir and for his sake, Amelia hoped he wouldn't wake up just yet.

"Have you come to gloat?" she asked.

Victoria paused, considering. "Well, I suppose so." She leaned against the bars, looking over each of them. "It is quite nice to see your enemies locked up in a cage, isn't it? There's a certain satisfaction."

"We're not your enemies."

"Well, honey, you're not my friends."

"Haven't you taken enough?" Amelia clenched her jaw. "I mean, why go to all this effort? Why did it have to be me? You had Emmaline. You almost had Harry. When will it be enough?" She recalled what Diana had told them. She tried to match the girl in front of her to the one she'd seen in that vision through Diana's eyes.

"Oh, Amelia, but that's the thing. This little *witch*—" Victoria pointed at Harriet— "she thought she could take what was mine. Just like you did. The magic alone wouldn't have been worth the trouble. Sure, taking your magic would have granted me more power than anyone alive could hardly *fathom*...but then you stole from me. And suddenly the scale tipped a little less in your favor. And then *she* stole from me. And it was over. All I needed was that wretch Emmaline. And she was just a tool."

"I didn't steal anything from you."

This seemed to make Victoria angry. "The *spoon*." Her voice was a low, ominous rumble. "The time loop. Remember?"

"There was nothing we could have done!" Sam protested.

"*Quiet!*" Victoria shot a finger in Sam's direction and the girl flinched in response.

Amelia didn't let it shake her. "We spoke to Emmaline."

Victoria looked back at her, waiting for her to go on.

"She told us about the hurt you caused. We saw it with our own eyes."

"Is that *all* she told you?"

Now it was Amelia who waited for her to elaborate.

And Victoria did. "Emmaline was a wicked girl. A bully. Sure, what I did was bad, but Emmaline would have pulled wings off of butterflies, so don't try to turn her into some sort of saint." She laughed to herself.

"Is that how you justify this, too?" Amelia asked. "Hunting us down? Terrorizing us? Hurting our friends? Because you figure we're bad, so we deserve it?"

For a moment, Victoria seemed to almost pity them. "I'm not as evil as you think I am. I do wish you could see past the black and white."

"Enough." It was Sofia who broke through their conversation. She had sat up straight, her expression serious and unwavering. "Enough of this. How did you get in here? What are you planning?"

And what Victoria said next, she said with a blunt simplicity that did the absurdity of her words absolutely no justice.

"I'm going to free you."

They all stared at her blankly.

"Why?" asked Sam.

Then, Amelia understood. "You can't take our magic until we leave the iron."

Victoria neither confirmed nor denied outright that this was the case. Instead, she plucked a small key from her pocket and clicked open the lock of Amelia and Sam's cell door. Then the other. Then she stood there, hands on hips, waiting.

Amelia wasn't sure how to react. The doors were open, yet they were far from free.

But then again, weren't they? They had no magic here, but neither did she. It was five of them against one of her—that is, once Peter woke up.

"All that big talk," Victoria mused. "You'll all be safe here. In theory. But you'll be at the mercy of the GMUC. Or..." she gestured to the open door, "you could leave. Walk out. And then we'll finally see."

"See what?" Amelia challenged.

"Which of us deserves the magic."

The magic within her. The magic suppressed somewhere at the base of her chest, waiting, dormant, unable to be summoned in this cell. She wanted to bite back, to tell her she had no right to what she was born with, that her magic was a deep-rooted part of her, that it was as integral as each of her lungs, that without it she could not breathe. But the words caught in her throat.

The girl before her was a wicked blend of features that resembled her mother so faintly—that resembled Amelia herself. She saw the woman who had already robbed her of her birthright once. She was the reason Amelia had been left in the dark about magic for the first fourteen years of her life. She was the reason her covenmates hadn't come into their own for nearly a year, turning them into near outcasts. So much suffering.

And here Victoria was, giving her the opportunity to put an end to it. An opportunity to prove herself. To find justice.

In the beginning, it had been about survival. She had wanted nothing more than to be done with Victoria. But now it was more. Now Amelia was angry.

"I'll go." Amelia moved forward.

Sam clutched her arm, holding her in place. "No."

"Yes." Amelia looked back at her and spoke softly. "You don't have to come."

"It's a trap. She's just trying to lure us in," Sam scoffed. "This is what she wants."

"I know."

"No, you don't know."

Amelia didn't respond at first. How could she tell Sam that she was doing this in part for her? If Amelia went, if she could finally prove herself, then she, too, could be free. They did not have to choose one of or the other—go or stay—they could choose both.

She reached up to Sam's face and grazed the side of her cheek, electricity running through her. It brought her back to that moment in the woods. The feel of Sam's lips against hers...

Sam brought Amelia's hand over her mouth, kissing her palm as she searched her expression with wide eyes. Her lips radiated heat.

"This is my fight," Amelia stated, and Sam's grip loosened. She could see in her eyes that she wanted to fight her, but she did not. Amelia's hand slowly fell away.

She turned back to Victoria.

"Let's go."

As she began to leave the cell, Sofia spoke.

"Amelia."

She paused.

Sofia stood against the bars, her gaze intense. Her voice was so quiet Amelia might have been the only one who heard it.

"You know who you are."

Amelia nodded tensely.

And then she was gone.

Once they had left the room, Victoria made Amelia spin around and then tied her hands behind her back with tape. "A bit of insurance," she told her, winking.

"I thought this was meant to be a fair fight."

"You'll get your moment, don't worry. But I can't have you running off."

They began to walk steadily down the hall. Each word echoed ominously off of the concrete, a dim gray lining all of the walls, each corner holding shadows that unnerved her. She studied Victoria at her side. What would scare her? So long Amelia had thought of this girl as the monster of her nightmares, some inhuman force, and yet here she stood, technically powerless, a normal person made of flesh and blood. Her skin was imperfect; there was a pimple on her chin. Her eyes were more tired than Amelia had realized. She had chipped nail polish and scattered moles on her arms just like Amelia. How old would she have been now? Nineteen? Seventeen?

Victoria must have a weakness. It was only a matter of finding it.

"We met Diana."

There was an almost imperceptible disturbance in the rhythm of Victoria's steps at Amelia's words. "In that case, perhaps I owe you an apology. I can't imagine she's any more bearable fifty years later." It was hard to tell if she was joking.

"She told us stories about you."

Victoria glanced in Amelia's direction and then took the bait. "Stories?"

"The two of you at the party in London. You in Melilla. The letters she sent you." She paused. "The day you got that power."

Victoria said no more, continuing down the winding hall. They had passed a couple other doors, all identical to the ones outside the witches' cell. Amelia wondered what they held.

She pushed harder. "She told us about Eloise, your coven-mate."

Victoria had ceased to react. Either she could tell what Amelia was doing, or she'd come to a dead end.

So she asked the same thing that she'd asked Diana.

"Did you love her?"

Without warning, Victoria grabbed Amelia by the collar and slammed her back against the wall. With her arms constrained, Amelia could do nothing to fight it. Air left her chest instantly and she coughed, choking as Victoria held her in the air. Even without magic, she was stronger than she looked. Her expression twisted into something terrifying, her teeth bared like fangs.

"Say that again and see what happens," she hissed.

"You're a coward!" Amelia cried.

Victoria gripped her tighter, fingers curling around her throat, and Amelia raised up her knee and drove it flat into her abdomen. Victoria's grip loosened and she doubled over. She raised her hands again, palms facing outwards, and for just a moment, it looked as if she intended to use her magic. But nothing came. She lowered her hands, cursing.

If there was one benefit to Amelia's fourteen years in the dark, it was this. She did not make the same mistake. Instead, hands still behind her back, she pulled back her leg and kicked Victoria square in the chest, quick enough to make her stumble back, her balance lost. Amelia then tackled her and they both toppled over. She twisted around and used one hand to loop her finger through Victoria's belt buckle, holding her in place, and the other to reach inside her pocket. Her skin found metal, and before Victoria could wrench her away, Amelia used her last handy trick.

She reeled her head back and butted it against Victoria's skull before rolling away.

And then she was on her feet and running, darting down the hall as fast as she could with both hands tied behind her, one held in a tight fist, metal keys digging into her palms. She came up to the closest iron door and took only a fraction of a second to look through the tiny glass window. *It'll have to do*, she thought before pressing her back to the door so that she could search for the keyhole with her fingers.

Victoria was coming back to the other side of the hall, rising to her feet. She began charging for Amelia, a low battle cry rising from her throat. Just then, Amelia found the hole and slid the key in. With a satisfying *click*, the door gave way and she fell inside.

She scrambled to close the door just before Victoria reached it. With a satisfying *SLAM*, the room was sealed and Victoria's raging cries were barely audible.

Amelia began to crumple, the exhaustion catching up on her as she panted heavily.

But then she realized that another rhythmic breath followed behind her own. She held her breath for a moment. Yes, a steady inhale and exhale sounded behind her. Air tickled the back of her neck.

She was not alone.

Slowly, she turned around.

An Unexpected Ally

"Hello," Amelia said.

"Hello," the creature in front of her replied, its head bumping against the ceiling with a metallic *clang*.

On the other side of the cell's iron bars was a monster.

It was familiar to her in every aspect besides its size. It looked remarkably similar to Jerry, the tiny gargoyle that lived in the secret room in Gloria's library back home. This one was much, much larger, but it had the same crooked overbite leading into sharp fangs, a swishing tail lined with spikes that followed all the way up its back, and every inch of it made of cold, hard stone. It did not blink, its eyes made of two round rocks below a furrowed, angry brow. A low sound rumbled from within the creature, somewhere between a growl and a purr.

"You're a gargoyle," Amelia said stupidly.

"Yes," the creature replied slowly, its voice deep and gravelly and not quite human. It leaned slightly closer, nearing the bars that separated them. "Gargoyle."

"Why are you so...large?"

"I one hundred and six," said the gargoyle in broken English. It pressed its nose to the bars and sniffed. "Why you...small?"

So, Jerry was a baby. Good to know.

Amelia gulped. "I'm fourteen."

"Hmmm," it purred.

"What's your name?"

"Bob."

"Will you help me, Bob?" Amelia could still distantly hear Victoria pounding at the door. She wondered how long it would be before she found a way in. As they spoke, she began using the key in her hand to pierce the tape holding her hands together.

"You key," said Bob.

Amelia broke the tape and her arms were free. She looked down at the keys in her hand. "Yes. I'll let you free."

"I help," the creature nodded languidly.

Amelia sighed a breath of relief. "Okay. I need you to distract her." She pointed at the door. "She's bad. Do you understand?"

Bob nodded.

Well, that was the level of certainty they were going to have to go with. With a steadying sigh, she brought the key to the cell's lock and opened the door.

She perhaps had not registered quite how big he was until then. With each step, the floor shook beneath them. He had to squeeze himself through the opening sideways before he was finally released and then there was hardly any space for Amelia, his form taking up the whole room. She wasn't even sure if he'd be able to make it through the door..

"Ready?" she asked him.

He nodded.

She stood behind the door and swung it open. Chaos erupted as Victoria charged into the room, radiating rage. She came up face to face with the gargoyle, who unhinged his jaw and let out a deafening bellow. Amelia slammed her hands over her ears but it was hardly enough. The creature snapped at Victoria and she went scrambling back out the door. Once again, she lifted her hands as if to use her magic but came up empty-handed. The gargoyle lunged for her and she had no choice but to flee, digging desperately for something in her back pocket.

Amelia took advantage of the moment and went running down the hall in the opposite direction, searching for a door that was different from the rest. She was looking for something sleek and white that matched the GMUC main hall, something that could take her—

She spotted it, just at the corner, almost hidden by shadow. She went running straight for it, the sounds of crashing, snarling, and violent slashing from behind her as the gargoyle and Victoria continued to fight. She approached the door and swung it open, her eyes shut as she envisioned the room where she wished to go...

When she opened her eyes it was there. The time machine. It stopped and started, spluttering with sparks and glitterings of magic. Someone had done something to it in the time they'd been gone. But still, she could feel that same pull to the room like before, that same proximity to magic through the wires that ran along the floor. But now she understood that the pull she felt was to the machine itself, as well. She was connected to it. Victoria had left some part to herself within it, and it was unnerving but also intriguing.

Okay. She took another deep breath but she knew she did not have long. She had gotten this far, and now was her moment. Now was her one opportunity. She got to work instantly, circling the machine, searching desperately for that one kink she had noticed before, the chip somewhere within that had drawn her attention. She grazed her fingers along the edge of the metal, getting a feel for it all, becoming one with it.

There! Her attention caught on a gap down in the depths of the engine. It wasn't an engine, really. It was like a heart, pumping magic from the wires up through the machine, veins crawling across every part of it. Every one of them led back here to this point. Amelia bent over, trying to get a look at it. If she could just get to it, she could fix what was missing and the machine would *finally* be functional and—

The door swung open. Victoria's hair was a frazzled mess, half covering her face. Only one wide and rabid eye was exposed, set firmly on Amelia. Bob the gargoyle was nowhere to be found. She was panting, her stance wide, but it was clear she was not finished yet.

Amelia could feel that one chance slipping away.

Although the magic that flowed through this room was not strong, it was enough for Victoria. Once again, she raised her hands, but this time they began to glow with that familiar purple aura, a color that matched Amelia's almost exactly. And just before the blast came, she was struck by the realization of just how similar they might really be.

Amelia was blinded by the light that shot towards her, but the machine stood between them, and she was able to dive out of the way behind it. The metal shuddered with the impact, but she saw no damage. Victoria may have been psychotic, but she was good at what she did.

"You don't want this!" Amelia shouted, scrambling to her feet.

"Oh, but I do," Victoria replied coolly, stalking around the machine, her steps controlled and poised, like a cat's. "For you, it's been a couple weeks. But me? I've been waiting for this for years. I've done nothing but plan and wait."

Amelia was standing now, still hidden behind the machine as Victoria circled around, hands pulsing with light. "Diana didn't want this," Amelia insisted.

"Diana is a goddamn fool."

"Diana *loves you!*"

Their eyes locked over the edge of the machine and Victoria swung her arms forward. Another blast of light came her way, but this time, Amelia did not dodge it. With one hand on the metal, she threw up her other and focused all her energy on the ball of light. With her magic, she cradled it and took it in before redirecting it in Victoria's direction. With the power moving through her from the wires and the machine, it went flying with greater force than she'd expected.

It nearly knocked Victoria off her feet. She skidded along the floor, but did not fall. It was clear that the older girl had never learned to dodge a blow, to run away from a fight. She took everything as it was because she believed she could handle it. And she had no reason to believe otherwise.

Victoria's form seemed to flicker and, instinctually, Amelia stopped time.

Victoria was at her side, inches from her, reaching for her. Amelia ducked out of the way. They had both stopped time, and now they were in sync. To any other person, they would have been nothing but a blur, but to each other, they were moving at the same speed.

Amelia focused her energy towards Victoria's knee and, with a sharp flick of her wrist, pushed it sideways.

As Victoria began to lose balance, Amelia went running the opposite way, dragging her hand across the machine, but then something strange happened. She was suddenly standing back where she'd been but a moment ago.

She tried to run again.

And then she was back in the same spot. Again.

Victoria yanked her by the neck from behind and Amelia gasped, choking. Her neck was hooked in the crook of Victoria's elbow and they began to rise up together, their feet leaving the floor. Magic swirled around them in a burst of glistening light. She could not see Victoria's face, but she heard her laugh with maniacal triumph.

"I should kill you now," said Victoria.

Amelia struggled against her grip, her legs kicking uselessly in the air. "*Nghh. No!*" she groaned, digging her fingernails into the girl's arms, but she didn't seem to notice.

"You're right," Victoria cooed. "I can do much worse."

Victoria dropped her and Amelia was weightless for a long moment. Then she hit a hard surface and her body was shot through with both pain and magic. Dizzy, she struggled to process her surroundings. She had landed flat on her back, directly on top of the time machine. The ringing in her head was from the impact with the metal casing and the magic sizzling against her back was from its internal components. Amelia reached for the power as Victoria landed on top of her, pinning her so that she couldn't move or focus.

And then she began to feel it. That exact thing which Harriet had described. Which Emmaline had described. The thing she had been most afraid of.

Her magic began to leave her. No, that was not the right way to describe it. Her magic was *wrenched* from the depths of her soul, seeping from every organ, sucked from her very veins. She couldn't breathe. It was her life force and Victoria was draining it. She felt herself turning into nothing, an empty husk, a hollow shell.

She reached for something, anything. The buzz of the machine still droned on against her back. She lurched toward it, flinging out her net wildly.

And she found something. Not within the machine, but within Victoria.

She recalled the witch hunter from the hostel who had fallen from the building. The man was not dead, but he had died. He had died because of Amelia.

She raised her hand and planted it on Victoria's chest above her, feeling the rise and fall of her breath. Victoria looked down, confused.

"I'm sorry," Amelia told her, and then began to pull.

The magic began to return to her, seeping in through her arm and then all throughout her body, hot and freezing at the same time, tingling beneath her skin. It was erratic and she wasn't sure if she could stop it even if she tried. She pulled harder and harder. Victoria tried to yank herself away but it was no use. They were both in it now.

She felt the moment Victoria tried again. The magic flowing into her began to resist. They were both trying to steal from the other at once.

Victoria began to laugh again, her voice harsh and manic. "You're just like me, Amelia!" she shouted over the deafening ring in both of their ears. Her cat-like grin was barely visible through the shine of magic swelling around them. It was a power manifested, the materialization of their terrible game of tug-of-war. "You'll never win, don't you see?"

Amelia pushed Victoria off of her, trying to separate them, but it was no use. They remained connected. A thread of light ran between them, glowing brighter and brighter, pushing and pulling between their bodies. She could not let go. Victoria would not.

"Just let me end this!" Amelia cried. "We have to stop!"

Victoria shook her head, her hands wrapping over the thread of magic between them. It kept growing, becoming bigger and brighter by the second. "It will be one of us. Or neither of us," she spat, but her smile remained. This was what she wanted. This battle. This intensity. Victoria had always intended to go down in flames.

Amelia gritted her teeth and gripped the thread that was now as thick as a rope. It sizzled against her palms as she pulled. The machine continued to shudder violently beneath them, like it could sense their conflict, like it was ready to combust with them.

"*No!*" Amelia screamed, her throat raw. "I'm not like you. I won't be!"

Victoria threw her head back and laughed.

But then Amelia spotted it from the edge of her vision. The door had cracked open. The corner of her mouth curled into a smile.

She looked back at Victoria. "I'm not," she said again. "I have what you never did."

Victoria opened her mouth, but Amelia never did find out what she had meant to say.

The world went dark and silent.

When the Past Comes Knocking

The rumbling of the machine beneath them ceased abruptly as the overhead lights went out. The buzz of magic through the room was cut off and everything was utterly empty. The thread of magic between Amelia and Victoria flickered once and was snuffed out completely. For a moment, Amelia was blind and clueless.

But then the lights came on again, everything around her bursting into color so bright she had to squint. The two of them were still balanced on top of the time machine. Amelia's gaze swept toward the entrance to the room and her heart leapt in her chest.

Sam was standing in the open doorway. Their gazes met and Sam moved forward. Amelia had the distinct thought just then that no matter where this girl was—anywhere in the world—Amelia would be able to find her.

Harriet came through the door behind Sam. Then Sofia. And Peter.

Elena appeared behind them, and Amelia was mildly confused but still happy.

Because she was right. She was not like Victoria. Victoria had thrown her coven away, not realizing it was her greatest strength.

With the power back on, Amelia's magic had returned, and this time she would not squander her opportunity to put an end to this. She gathered all the magic within her and sent a blast of energy towards Victoria. She cried out with effort, using all her might.

Elena ran to the base of the machine and raised her arms up, focusing her own power towards Victoria. Harry and Sofia came to stand beside her, echoing her pose. It was no longer a fair fight, and Victoria was overpowered. She staggered backward, her feet dangerously close to the edge of the machine.

Victoria slipped over the edge but caught herself, levitating above the floor.

There was movement at the doorway and Amelia immediately recognized Isabel. Though she looked just like Elena, the difference between them was clear now. Her face was twisted with rage. "*Elena!*" she screamed. "What have you done?"

From behind her, Stephanie and Gloria stepped through the door.

Amelia blanched. "*Mom?* What are you doing here?" As for Gloria, she couldn't even begin to imagine how the vampire had ended up here with them.

"I got a call." Stephanie's face was laced with concern. She looked as if she wanted to scoop Amelia up right then and there, but Amelia was still perched on top of the machine and Victoria was still there, hovering above the ground as she looked upon them all.

Victoria's gaze darkened and her lips moved to mouth the word Amelia had used. *Mom.*

Amelia crouched down at the edge of the machine's metal roof and extended one leg over the side. She gripped one of the ridges that ran along the top and lowered her weight to land gently on her feet. She moved towards her mother and the others until they all stood together, united. She looked back at Victoria with a stony glare.

"Don't you see?" she asked her. "This is what you've missed."

Victoria's lips curled into a cruel snarl. She moved forward, as if to lunge again, but another voice cut through the room.

"She's right, Vic."

The witch froze. All of the blood seemed to leave her face as she turned to the corner.

Diana stood there, her pained expression forming deep wrinkles in her tired skin. She closed the bottle of bubbles in her hands and tucked it away in her cardigan pocket. She didn't speak for a moment. Neither of them did, staring at each other with the weight of forty years hanging between them.

How did Victoria look to Diana? How strange must it have been for the woman to look upon her covenmate who she had not seen for so long? To look upon her love whom she'd lost, not a day older?

And how did Diana look to Victoria? It was clear in her face that she recognized her. But how *different* she must have looked. How strange and painful that moment must have been for them both. Amelia could not even begin to understand.

And yet Victoria could only manage one word.

"Traitor."

Isabel stepped toward Victoria and raised her arms, summoning a waft of clouds and wind around her. The ceiling began to turn into a sky, electricity and lighting crackling above their heads.

If this was how the witch's capabilities looked when dulled by the iron, Amelia couldn't imagine what her powers could be at full strength.

"Surrender now, Lake!" she shouted in Victoria's face.

Victoria blinked slowly. Isabel's magic seemed to be the least of her worries. "You're all pathetic."

She lunged toward Isabel. With one foot hooked beneath a wire to maintain her grip on her power, Victoria shoved both hands against Isabel's chest, throwing the woman backward like a ragdoll. Isabel cried out and the clouds above flickered weakly. Her back hit the wall and she groaned in pain.

Elena responded immediately, throwing up illusions from every angle, but it wasn't enough, not in that room. Victoria was not fooled. She sent another blast towards Elena, who was able to dodge it, but she was visibly shaken.

Harriet and Sofia stepped forward next, their powers glowing side by side. Sofia bent down to the ground, gripping one of the wires with her hand. Vines began to break through the concrete floor, bursting up and curling around Victoria's legs. She slashed at them but they moved quickly, catching on her clothes, pulling at her limbs. Harriet, meanwhile, was moving a gust of wind around the room, blowing Victoria's blonde curls into her face, blinding her.

Suddenly, Victoria vanished, as if she'd never been there at all.

Amelia stopped time. It took more effort than usual, but she understood the mechanics of it better now. She just needed to push a little harder.

Beside her, Victoria was lunging for a frozen Sofia. Amelia shoved Victoria away with a gust of magic and grabbed Sofia's hand, unfreezing her. The witch hardly needed direction.

Hand in hand, they began to fight Victoria again, sending blasts of magic, deadly plants, and blinding flashes towards her.

Seeing it was useless, and slowly running out of energy, Victoria released her hold on time and it collapsed back into normal speed. The room erupted into movement again. Isabel and Elena were back on their feet. All around them, everyone was throwing one deadly spell after another. Amelia was barely thinking, only reacting. All she could think about was destroying Victoria, putting an *end* to it and—

One of Victoria's spells flew past Amelia, nearly catching her on the shoulder. There was a crash behind her and a voice cried out. Amelia spun.

Her mother was on the ground, her body limp and motionless. Gloria was at her side in an instant, cradling her head. But she was still. Too still.

Amelia felt all energy, all drive leave her. Her stomach dropped and every inch of her skin went cold. It couldn't be true.

Stephanie's eyes were locked on the ceiling, glazed over and glassy. Amelia knew that look. She'd seen it on Sam's father. On Manon.

No. Gloria clutched her like a delicate treasure and her gaze rose to meet Amelia's.

Red prickled at the edges of Amelia's vision. She turned back to Victoria and there was only red. As if it was playing out through a movie screen, Amelia lifted her hand, letting it shine with a lethal and bright aura. A spell left her lips, ancient words she didn't recognize.

Victoria was staring down at Stephanie. Was she finally realizing who the woman on the floor was? Perhaps it was their identical curly hair or the look on Amelia's face. Perhaps she had already known, and it had been an accident.

It didn't matter. Amelia let the magic flow.

And then it was Victoria who was thrown violently across the room, her head whipping back before she slammed against the floor. Her body came alight with Amelia's spell and then she stilled.

It took a moment for Amelia's vision to clear, for her breath to steady. Diana knelt beside Victoria's body. She held a finger at her neck, checking her pulse.

She removed her hand, her composure slipping.

"She's dead."

A Death in the Family

Amelia Aubert did not cry when her grandmother died for the second time.

She was shaking with rage, with sadness, with desperation. She could not bear to look towards her mother on the other side of the room. It was like she was the one frozen in time now. She knew she should go to her, she should see if what she thought was really true. But she'd watched life go out of Manon's eyes as they both remained helpless to what was happening. And she couldn't do it all over again. She wouldn't.

No.

She could turn back time, Amelia remembered desperately. She lifted her arms and tried to get a grip on it—tried with all her might to focus her energy like she had when she'd sent a blast towards Victoria. She felt around with her magic, trying to twist it backwards as she had twice before, but it was not the same. Her magic would not act in the way she wanted, it would not comply. Even when she pressed a hand to the machine, absorbing its energy, she could not bend it to her will.

Amelia fell to her knees. All of her strength was gone. She wanted to allow herself to crumble and sink into the floor. A heavy weight sat on her chest, suffocating her. She couldn't even draw out a sob. It would not come.

"Amelia."

She looked up, reeling.

Gloria stood above her, a hand on her shoulder. Her eyes were flashing a deep red, her skin bright. She was as beautiful as the first time Amelia had seen her in the library, with soft, black waves curling down her shoulders, her lips painted a dark, cool red.

"I can bring her back," Gloria said softly, her voice smooth.

"What?" Amelia tried to straighten but didn't have the will.

"I can turn her. She has magic in her blood."

Amelia tried to speak but no sound came out.

"She'll be immortal," Gloria explained. "She will live forever. Longer than you. Longer than everyone she loves. And she will be inhumanly powerful. But she will be dead. As dead as I am."

"You mean make her a vampire," Amelia managed to utter weakly.

Gloria nodded. "But I need you to tell me that's what you want, my dear. We have limited time before she's gone forever."

Amelia could not imagine a world in which her mother did not exist. She could not live. The world would surely cease to spin, the birds to sing. So many things had changed in the last months. But this was too much.

But was it what Stephanie would want? She had always been resilient, but could she be immortal? And who was

Amelia, truly, to decide? How could she possibly be worthy of laying out her own mother's entire future?

For a moment, there was nothing but silence.

The word left her lips with no logic behind it, no reason. "Yes."

So Gloria did it. She bent over Stephanie and carefully sunk her teeth into the side of her neck. Everyone in the room watched as she injected vampire venom into her veins, cradling her head gently, as if it were nothing but a kiss. And then she pulled away, leaning her body propped gingerly against the wall.

And they waited. It took long minutes, during which none of them said a single word. When Amelia glanced towards Victoria's body, she saw Diana still kneeling at her side, cradling her cheek with her hand. Amelia looked away.

Stephanie's lashes fluttered. Slowly, blood began to creep back into her face. Her lips were turning pink. Gloria made a small cut in her wrist and raised it to Stephanie's mouth. She took the offering without opening her eyes, sucking hungrily from the pale skin.

When Stephanie's eyes finally opened, they were red.

She sat up, looking around with a certain alertness she hadn't had before. "Mellie."

Her voice had a different cadence to it than before. It was still the same Amelia had been hearing for the past fourteen years, but there was something about the *way* she'd said her nickname. Something had most definitely changed.

Amelia didn't care. She ran to her mother and dropped down to the floor beside her. She gripped both her hands, looking deep into her red eyes. "Mom," she sobbed. "You're alive."

"I..." Stephanie looked around, as if to test the truth of this statement. "Yes."

Amelia's head fell onto her mother's shoulder and she began to cry. They were powerful, heaving sobs ripped from deep within her, a sound she'd never made before. Her mother gently stroked her chocolate curls and they held each other tightly. When her sobs finally dwindled, Amelia inhaled the smell of her mother, buried deep within her hair. She smelled like home, like old books and breakfast pancakes. But there was something else now, too, something sharp and old-fashioned. She smelled...like Gloria.

"We have to revive her." Isabel's voice echoed from behind them.

Amelia pulled away and turned. "What?"

Isabel was standing over Diana and Victoria's body. "We must find a way to revive Victoria."

"No," Amelia choked out. "No, it's *over.*"

Isabel's expression was stony and serious. "I would not suggest it if it were not necessary. But if she stays like this, then everything leading up to this moment will not have happened. She won't marry, she won't have a child, and her child won't have a child. And then Harry and Sofia won't be witches, and neither of you will exist."

Isabel's gaze had gone intense. "Do you understand, Amelia? If she dies, so do you and your mother. This must be done and it must be done quickly."

Amelia paused, thinking. They couldn't turn Victoria into a vampire, certainly. No fate was worse than one where she had that kind of power. And there was no healing potion in the world that could bring her back to life from where she was now, lying lifeless in Diana's arms.

Amelia stood, unsure of what she planned to do. But something within her knew. Something within her guided her forward to kneel beside Diana.

Diana raised her head. There were tears drying across her cheeks, her expression still contorted with an old, dying pain.

Amelia placed her hand over Diana's. She understood now—this was her peace. This was her closure. All those years of sending letters, of never really knowing what had truly happened to her covenmate, now she could see it all first hand. Now, she could say goodbye.

She hoped Diana knew that she understood the way she felt. She hoped she knew she was eternally grateful for the help she'd offered.

Amelia's hand slowly shifted from Diana's down to Victoria's chest, which did not rise and fall with any breath. Distantly, she was aware of all the eyes on her now, waiting to see what she would do.

With her other hand, Amelia touched the wire and felt magic run through her. That push and pull that she'd gone through with Victoria—it had changed something inside her, too. They had exchanged something, and not all the magic in Amelia was her own.

Then she did something which had never occurred to her to do before.

She gave it back.

The magic that she'd taken, the small spark of Victoria's magic left inside her, she pushed it back through her hands and into the witch's chest. She glowed brightly, feeling it all pass through her. She felt a great relief as she returned what was not hers.

Victoria took in a breath. Her chest rose and Amelia pulled back. She seemed to glow, her eyes fluttering open with life.

Diana gripped her tightly, holding the back of her head.

"Vic? Vic, how do you feel?"

Victoria coughed. "I feel...great." She paused and looked up, finally processing who exactly she was looking at. It wasn't *her* Diana. And it must have been that sight which snapped her back into focus. She moved to sit back up but suddenly, Sofia's vines which had been lying limply across the floor, tensed and wrapped themselves around her limbs, holding her in place. Before she could act, Isabel came around behind her and placed both hands on her temples. In an instant, the witch relaxed back into Diana's arms, her expression going foggy.

"I'm not sure you all will want to see this," Isabel warned.

"What are you going to do?" asked Diana, still holding her covenmate tightly.

"I'm going to wipe her memory."

None of them noticed that Stephanie had risen, and now stood over them, studying Victoria. There was an emotion on her face that Amelia couldn't identify. She looked pained.

"How much of it?" Stephanie asked softly.

"Not all of it," Isabel replied. "Enough for her to forget the details of her past. We'll send her to the States, and she'll live her life as she...well, as she already did."

Stephanie was silent for another moment. "So, this is how it always was?"

"What do you mean?" asked Amelia.

A wistful smile lined her lips. "All those times I pried. I tried to get her to tell me about her past, to teach me about magic, but she treated the subject with such sensitivity I grew afraid to ask. But I guess this makes sense. She didn't understand most of it herself. She didn't remember."

Isabel nodded gravely as she worked.

"And she didn't reply to my letters," murmured Diana. "All those years."

"It's why she left me the chest," said Amelia suddenly, realizing. "She wasn't leaving it as a code or a test. She didn't keep it from me on purpose."

Diana finished her thought for her. "She hoped you would make sense of it."

It was strange; looking down at Victoria, speaking of things in the past tense that she would do in the future.

"It's the only way we maintain the timeline," said Isabel. "Without her hurting anyone else."

Everyone agreed. Even Diana, though it pained her. The air in the chamber grew heavy as Isabel worked. Threads of light spilled from her fingertips, winding delicately through Victoria's temples, sinking into her skin like smoke into stone. The others watched in silence—Sofia keeping her vines taut, Diana clutching her covenmate like she was holding onto the last fragment of a memory.

Victoria's whitened eyes fluttered. Her expression softened, slackened, until the sharp edge of recognition was gone. She breathed evenly now, almost peacefully, as if she had only just been roused from a long sleep.

"It's done," Isabel whispered, finally lowering her hands. A weariness touched her shoulders, but her eyes remained steady. "She will not remember us. Not the fight. Not the machine. Not the power she wielded. To her, this will all be a dream she never had." She looked up at Amelia. "You did well. You did what should not have been possible."

For a long moment, none of them moved. The air was thick, filled only with Victoria's quiet breaths and the steady hum of the currents running through the room.

Diana smoothed a strand of hair from Victoria's face and then bent down, pressing a gentle kiss to her temple. Amelia's gaze fell on Sam, who came closer, as if summoned, and wrapped her arms around her. They leaned into each other, comforted by the familiar warmth.

Stephanie shifted beside them, her voice softer than before. "She'll have her life. And we'll have ours. How it was always meant to be." But she looked down at her own hands, which had grown pale, skin pulled tight over the tendons.

No one disagreed.

Amelia glanced at her companions, her chest aching but lighter than it had been in days. Everything had changed, yet somehow remained exactly the same. They'd been through so much, only to end up back where they'd started, preserving the past to keep this future. To keep each other.

The glow of the spell slowly faded from the air, leaving the room washed in the ordinary stillness of the aftermath. And as they gathered themselves to leave—supporting one another, quiet and solemn—Amelia cast one last look at Victoria.

She would not remember the way this had ended, not the love and grief tangled between each of their stories.

But Amelia would.

Today, Yesterday, and Tomorrow

The following days were quieter than any of them expected. They had anticipated endless interrogations from the GMUC, maybe even from the witch news outlets that had become obsessed with uncovering the department's secrets, and yet, to their surprise, Isabel and Elena had seen to it that they be left alone. And so the house remained still. The coven had nothing but each other. And Peter, of course.

But strangely, that was plenty.

A weight had been lifted from Amelia's chest. She held Sam's hand whenever she had the chance. She continued her banter with Harriet, and they all teased Sofia—but it was alright, because she knew full well they all loved her. And though Peter did not live at the house with them (he had taken up residence with Oscar's parents as his host family) they had accepted him into their circle and he was a frequent visitor. He and Harriet were growing closer. There was some sort of shared understanding between them that Amelia could not quite identify but was nevertheless supportive of.

Her mother was now much more accustomed to the concept of using magic and began to teleport over to Spain. After all, she didn't have much of a choice. But being newly immortal did have its perks when it came to confidence.

Stephanie was different. But she was still Amelia's mother. They continued to do all the things that they had done before Amelia discovered she was a witch; they watched a movie on the sofa every now and then; they cooked questionable food and made the other taste-test their creation (because, fortunately, while vampires did live off of blood, animal or human, they wouldn't get sick from a couple bites of a pineapple pizza either); they bickered and fought sometimes but then laughed about it soon afterwards. If anything, it seemed to make them closer, because now Stephanie could finally *get it.* Amelia was not the only strange one. She didn't have to translate everything into a language her mother would understand.

Plus, they could both move at super-speed now, which was cool.

The only weird part was that it seemed her mother's presence was a package-deal, for every time Stephanie visited, she had Gloria in tow. Amelia was still mildly suspicious about that relationship.

"I won't have to call you mom, too, will I?" Amelia asked the vampire one day while she was forced to sit between her and her mother on the sofa while they watched a horror movie. Stephanie had left the room to get more popcorn.

Gloria had only grinned to herself, flashing fang as she turned back to the screen.

But there was one other issue which arose as she sat with her coven on the carpet one afternoon, playing a card game that was bound to turn violent if Harriet picked up one more bad card.

"But you should have seen her, Amelia," said Sam as she recalled that day in the GMUC when Elena had broken them all out of their cell. "She was all like *I'm tired of being pushed around by you, Isa! They deserve better! Take that! Hi-yah!*"

"She might be exaggerating," chimed Sofia as she took another card from the deck.

Amelia didn't care. She was simply pleased to see Sam so animated again. That bounce in her step had returned, the ease with which she always said and did things, that bright smile that had made Amelia love her so.

"I don't think I've ever been more glad to see anyone in my life as I was when you all walked in the door," Amelia said, gently stroking Percy, who sat contentedly in her lap. "When you turned off the lights, it was a stroke of genius! How did you even think of it?"

"What do you mean?" asked Harriet, tossing a nut up into the air before catching it in her mouth.

"When you turned off the power." Amelia was met with confused silence. Percy mewled irritatedly at her for she had stopped petting him. "And magic stopped flowing through the machine. So the tie between me and Victoria broke."

"What are you talking about?" asked Sam. "We never turned off the power."

"But...I saw you walk in just then. You were the first one inside."

Sam shrugged. "The lights were on when I walked in."

"But then who..." Amelia trailed off. It took a moment for it all to come to her. For her to understand. But then it fell into place. What they had been missing from that day.

There was still one final piece to the story.

Amelia did not need to break into the GMUC the next time she visited. In fact, she had an esteemed officer of the Police Department of Magic right by her side as the elevator lowered.

Elena had spoken her name smoothly to the telepath operator in the mirror. (A new one, of course. The last one had been fired very, very quickly.) And then, once they were granted access, it was easy for them to find their way back to that room where it had all happened.

The chamber that held the time machine hadn't changed much. She'd heard they'd stripped some of the funding that went into its repair, and so their work had slowed, but magic continued to flow into it. They had not yet given up.

"I let them know you'd be coming today, so they cleared the room," Elena told her as they stood before the machine. "Some of the Casters got a bit excited, actually. You'd be surprised at the name the Hummingbird Coven has made for itself around here."

"You mean they...like me?" Amelia didn't mean to get so flattered.

"Well, I may have let slip what a natural you are. With a gift like that, dear, how could I not?" She looked down at her, smirking. "I have a feeling you'll do great things. And I'm not the only one." She paused, running her fingers along the loose wires of the machine. "In fact, perhaps one day you'd like to take on a couple assignments here at headquarters? And maybe one day on the field with me?" She nudged her.

Amelia hesitated. "I'll think about it."

But she knew she wouldn't. The thought of it was enough to make her chest feel heavy.

Glory here came at a cost, and she had no intention of paying it.

Elena gave her a long, quiet look, then smiled knowingly.

"That's what I thought."

Amelia soon got to work, and Elena sat and watched her as she tinkered with the large machine, handing her tools and offering assistance when she needed it. Figuring out the issue was not the difficult part, but Amelia was not quite as handy as she aspired to be, and so putting her repairs into practice took a solid hour.

But finally, after tears and sweat and a lot of smudge on her face, it was done. The second she finished, she could sense the energy shift around her. The magic and power that flowed through the wires now seemed to do so more smoothly. That dormant pulse that rested expectantly within the time machine was stronger. It was ready for her.

"Okay." She took a deep breath, steadying herself.

"Are you ready?" Elena asked her.

"Yup," Amelia lied.

"Turning on now." Elena flipped the switch and the entire machine came alive, stuttering and blubbering awkwardly at first, but then settling into a slow and even hum. The opening at the front of it glowed purple, welcoming her in.

"No time like the present," Amelia muttered, and then stepped inside.

There was no feeling quite like being yanked through both time and space. But Amelia quickly understood why no one but her could have navigated through the contraption. Although Victoria had attempted to create a device that would work even for those without her magic, it was so purely *her*.

Once Amelia was inside, she found herself floating between the timelines, purple strings weaving around her. The threads were constantly in motion, each one nearly identical to the last. If Amelia were less familiar with her own magic, she might have been lost, but the path was clear to her now. She grabbed the thread she needed and followed along its length before identifying the right spot and sinking into it.

And then she was stepping out of the machine, back in the same chamber as before.

But now, there was a deafening roar from above. When she moved further from the machine she could see that above it, two figures were balanced, a glowing line of magic pulsing between them. They fought with an endless push and pull of power, both grunting with the effort.

It had been several days now since Amelia had seen Victoria. She had expected to have more of a reaction at the sight of her face. And yet she didn't. The pain she felt for her was a dull one, one she was already learning to live with. This part of her life was over.

Amelia could not see her own face as her past self battled with Victoria, only her brown curls and purple aura.

She turned away. She had only one mission here in the past.

After a moment's search, she spotted the powerbox that connected to each and every wire running through the chamber and to the machine. She made her way to it and grabbed the handles as Victoria and past-Amelia shouted to each other viciously over the chaos.

She pulled all the levers down. The world went completely dark. The magic settled and the tie between them broke.

Amelia pulled the levers back up.

Then, she turned around and left back through the opening of the machine—just as Sam walked into the room.

She found herself back in that limbo between timelines. She began to drift towards her own, ready to return to Elena.

Ready to go back home. She paused. Another string caught her eye.

Without thinking, she grabbed hold of it and settled on the thin line for a moment, studying it.

Did she want to know?

Hesitantly, she moved into it.

Amelia blinked against the sudden quiet, her breath catching as she realized she was no longer in the GMUC workshop.

The room smelled faintly of motor oil and dust. Concrete walls stretched out around her, their surfaces bare except for a few faded posters curling at the corners. Old shelves lined one side of the garage, cluttered with tools, scraps of metal, and jars filled with bolts and washers. A workbench sat beneath a small window, its surface littered with sketches and half-finished contraptions.

The time machine itself sat awkwardly in the center of it all, its bulk oddly out of place in a room meant for cars and bicycles. Instead of gleaming with official polish as it had in the government's underground chamber, here it looked worn and patched, a vessel of secrets and stubborn perseverance. Parts of its frame were reinforced with ordinary wires and duct tape. There was even an open box of mismatched screws beside it.

A single bulb swung from the ceiling, casting long shadows that made the corners of the garage feel deeper than they were. Somewhere beyond the garage door came the muffled hum of the world—birds, maybe a car on the street, the faint whistle of wind.

Amelia's pulse quickened. She had the strange, unshakable sense of being expected. Something about all this was familiar.

And then the door opened.

She gasped. She could not help herself.

A child came running through, a little girl of about four stepping clumsily over the threshold. She had red curly hair and a smile that lit up the room when she spotted Amelia. She raced across the room, bordering on a waddle, and wrapped her arms around Amelia's legs.

"*Mommy.*"

And then another voice came, a shout from a distant room.

"Amelia?"

She recognized that voice.

It was Sam.

"Amelia, shake a leg! We need to leave now to meet Harry and Peter at the dock."

Sam, but older. More mature. Her tone had turned gravely and deep. It made Amelia feel warm all over. She was already on the verge of tears.

And then someone responded.

"Here!"

A woman passed by the garage door and caught sight of them. She stopped suddenly, her mouth falling slightly agape. She was tall and had a head of deep chocolate curls, pulled back at the nape of her neck, a few strands of gray in them, just like Stephanie wore hers. She had brown almond eyes and tawny, sun-kissed skin. She was wearing the necklace Sam had gifted her for her birthday.

Amelia was too stunned to move.

Her older self stepped into the garage and the little girl turned and ran to her just as she had to Amelia, and they turned away and began to leave.

But just before they did, the older Amelia glanced over her shoulder.

She held a finger to her lips and winked.

www.ingramcontent.com/pod-product-compliance
Lightning Source LLC
Chambersburg PA
CBHW030904060726

47591CB00005B/1409